W9-AYN-347

SCARY!

SCARY!

Stories That Will Make You SCREAM!

Edited by

PETER HAINING

BARNES
&NOBLE
BOOKS
NEW YORK

Copyright © 1998 by Seven Zenith Ltd.

This edition published by Barnes & Noble, Inc.,
by arrangement with Souvenir Press Ltd.

All rights reserved. No part of this book may be
used or reproduced in any manner whatsoever
without written permission of the Publisher.

1999 Barnes & Noble Books

ISBN 0-7670-1574-2 *casebound*
ISBN 0-7670-2311-7 *paperback*

Printed and bound in the United States of America

00 01 02 MC 9 8 7 6 5 4 3
00 01 02 MP 9 8 7 6 5 4 3 2 1

RRD-H

For
Richard, Sean and Gemma
and scaremongers everywhere

'We shall be very sorry when we've killed Olivia,' said the girl, 'but we can't be sorry till we've done it.'

Saki (H. H. Munro)
The Penance (1919)

CONTENTS

THE SCAREMONGERS

An Introduction

There is a story I read many years ago which I still believe is one of the neatest *and* scariest I've ever heard. It appeared in a book with the title *Across the Stream*, written by a ghost-story writer named E.F. Benson who specialised in frightening people. The story is told by a little boy called Archie who appears in the novel, and it's a murder mystery that really only needs a couple of red herrings to be perfect. You might like to put them in for yourself after you've read it:

> There was once a merderer with yellow eyes, and his wife said to him, 'If you merder me, you will be hung.' And he was hung on Tuesday next.

Stories about murder, horror and the supernatural have been popular with all ages for many years—it's something about being scared and enjoying it all at the same time. I know that's how I felt when I first discovered a book called *Spook Stories* almost fifty years ago (which, I'm afraid, shows just how old I am!), but my pleasure in reading them has never got any less.

At the moment, the horror stories of the American writer R.L. Stine are the biggest thing. But there is actually nothing really new about his kind of tale in which boys and girls find themselves in scary situations. A hundred and fifty years ago an author called Edgar Allan Poe was sending chills up the spines of anyone with nerves strong enough to read his stories like 'The Black Cat', 'The Murders in the Rue Morgue' and 'The Premature Burial'. Fifty years ago, H.P. Lovecraft launched a new craze for stories about beast men and horrifying monsters in stories such as 'The Haunter of the Dark', 'The Lurking Fear' and 'The Horror in the Burying Ground'.

More recently still, Roald Dahl and Stephen King have become huge favourites. Both have put children in a lot of frightening places in their books and stories. Stephen King even has an idea for one that he hasn't yet written. It seems he was talking to a journalist a couple of years ago when he mentioned an idea that had been buzzing around in his head— and I for one would love him to put it into words. 'You know those kiddies' rides in shopping precincts?' he said. 'Well, what would happen if a mother put her kid inside a ride, dropped in a coin, and watched the thing spin around a few times, and when it stopped, she discovered her son had disappeared?'

All the writers in this book have ideas about 'what happened next'. The kids in their stories are all very different, and you'll discover that they each have their own ways of handling the terrifying things that happen to them. The stories are a mixed bag of horror, fantasy, murder, mystery, detection and science fiction. Some of them even have mums, dads and grandparents who try to help—or more often than not just hinder. A few of the adults are even directly responsible for the dreadful events that occur . . .

I hope the stories will give you shivers rather than nightmares. But there's no guarantee, once you've passed this point—for The Scaremongers know their business only too well . . .

Peter Haining
February 1998

THE SPELL

R.L. Stine

*William is a serious, intense kid who seems to miss out most
of the time. He's always the object of Marty's teasing whenever the joker is showing off to the group of friends that
includes William's girlfriend, Jennifer. But Jennifer sees
something in William that the others don't—especially when
he gets interested in hypnotism and hides away in his attic
to study some books he's found in a grungy old bookstore.
It all gets really scary when William discovers that there's
a lot more to hypnotism than just reading books . . .*

*   *   *

I know I should call the police about William. But
I'm just sitting here staring at the phone. It's as if
someone has cast a spell over me or something.

William will be here soon. I don't know what
he's going to do to me. I really should call the
police.

But I keep thinking this just isn't the way it's supposed to be. I mean, we were all such good friends.
All five of us.

Erica and Stan were my friends first. But when I
started going out with William, it was like the four
of us had been close forever. Marty, too. Sure, Marty
was always teasing William, always making jokes,

always giving William a hard time. But Marty was like that with everyone.

With his curly red hair and his chubby, freckled face, his laughing blue eyes, Marty was a real Huck Finn type. You just had to like Marty. And even William, who is so serious, so earnest, so . . . intense, thought Marty was a great guy.

At first, anyway.

The five of us went to all the basketball games together. And we used to drive out on the River Road in Stan's old Pontiac and just hang out at the Falls, sitting in the tall grass, watching the water trickle over the rocks or staring up at the slow-drifting clouds.

Sometimes we had impromptu softball games there on the flat grass on the other side of the road. It was usually Stan and Erica against William, Marty and me. Long, lanky Stan was so good in sports, he and Erica usually won even though we outnumbered them.

Stan was so funny about the baseball bat he always brought. He claimed it really had belonged to Pete Rose during his rookie season in Cincinnati, and Stan treasured it. When we batted with it, he was always yelling at us to make sure the label was up so we wouldn't crack it.

William didn't like our softball games. He isn't very athletic. Sometimes when it was William's turn to bat, I'd actually see a glint of fear in those strange, slate-grey eyes of his.

He usually struck out. Or sent a weak grounder to the pitcher and was tagged out at first. And then Marty would really get on William's case. We all thought it was very funny. And William was always a good sport about all the ribbing. At least he didn't *seem* to mind.

One really hot Saturday afternoon, William hit the ball up, a high fly that sailed over Marty's head and kept going. William just stood open-mouthed, staring at it. He'd never hit the ball that far before.

'Run, William! Get moving!' I shouted. And then I saw that Marty was chasing the ball, running at full speed, staring straight up, his glove outstretched, his sneakers pounding on the ground. He chased it right into the river, made a desperate dive for it, but just missed.

What a splash he made. When he came up sputtering, he gazed into his glove. He couldn't believe he hadn't made the catch.

Before I realised what was happening, the four of us were running into the river to join Marty. The water was freezing! And our sopping-wet clothes weighed a ton. But we had so much fun ducking each other and splashing, tackling each other and mainly acting crazy.

That was one of the best days of my life.

I'm not sure when things started to go wrong.

It may have been when William got so interested in hypnotism. This was about the same time that Marty got the lead in the school musical, *The Music Man*. A major disappointment for William.

William is really very shy. He usually speaks very quietly, and he blushes easily. But he can be very intense, too. Those weird grey eyes of his light up, and he starts to talk very rapidly, very excitedly, raking his large hands back through his long, wavy, white-blond hair.

What I'm saying is that William has a theatrical side, too. I guess that's part of the reason he became so interested in hypnotism. He can be very dramatic, and there's a side of him that likes to show off.

That's why I wasn't surprised when he stopped me at my locker on the day of *The Music Man* auditions and said, 'Jennifer, I can't go home with you this afternoon. I've decided to try out.'

William really wanted to be the star. It meant he had to compete with Marty, who had been in the Drama Club all year, and who the drama coach thought was wonderful. Marty was just so popular.

But William auditioned anyway. And then when Marty got the part—big surprise!—William never talked about it again.

About a month later, Erica, Stan and I went to see Marty in the play. He was really good. William said he wasn't feeling well, so he didn't come.

None of us saw William as much as before—not even me. He was so involved with his hypnotism studies. He had stacks of old books about it that he had bought from some grungy bookstore downtown.

I have to admit I was a little hurt that he was spending more time up in that attic room of his, poring over those dusty, old books, than he spent with me. I tried to get interested in it, too. In fact, I begged William to show me what he was learning. But he stared at me and shook his head. He didn't want to share any of it.

Of course, Marty teased William about the hypnotism right from the start. Marty started calling him 'The Great Foodini', and he joked that William would soon start making us all bark like dogs and cluck like chickens. Then he'd start chasing William around, barking at him, nipping at him like a crazed puppy.

We all thought it was funny. I don't think any of us realised how seriously William took his hypnotism. I could see that he tensed up when Marty started giving him a hard time. But even I didn't realise what an angry person William was becoming.

I didn't even pick up on it when Marty got the part-time job in that Italian restaurant, the job William had also interviewed for.

All five of us were studying at my house the night Marty got the job. I saw William's eyes go cold, as cold and clear as ice. But he didn't say anything until Marty left. Then he turned to me and said under his breath, 'I really needed that job.'

Erica overheard and quickly said, 'So did Marty. His folks have been on his back for months to get a job.'

'Why do you stick up for *him?*' William screamed at her. I was shocked by his sudden anger.

'I—I wasn't,' Erica stammered.

'Give Erica a break,' Stan said. He'd been twirling that Pete Rose bat of his in the corner, but he quickly came to her defence.

'Everyone gives Marty a break,' William insisted with astonishing bitterness. 'Why doesn't anyone ever give *me* a break?' Then he grabbed his jacket off the floor and stormed out without looking back, slamming the kitchen door behind him.

After that, things really changed. The five of us just weren't comfortable together any more. Marty spent most nights working at the restaurant. I still saw Erica and Stan, but we didn't hang out as much as we used to. And William was spending more and more time in his attic, working on whatever it was he was working on.

I still cared about him a lot. He was so much more interesting than other guys, so much . . . deeper. But I was really worried about how distant he was becoming. He seemed so unhappy.

One Friday night the four of us were at a local hangout called the Pizza Palace, and William seemed in a really good mood. Marty was working. We talked about driving over and surprising him. Then the subject got changed to William and his hypnotism. I guess we were all teasing him about it. But for once, William was laughing, too.

'Let's try an experiment,' he suddenly suggested, smiling and jumping to his feet. He made Erica, Stan and me squeeze together on one side of the booth. 'Let's see if I really can hypnotise you,' he said.

All three of us immediately started clucking like chickens. We were laughing and goofing around. I felt more than a little nervous. I mean, I wondered what it felt like to be hypnotised.

William held up a teaspoon and told us to relax and follow it with our eyes. Erica had to hold her hand over her mouth to stop giggling. I think she was nervous, too.

Eventually, we all settled down and followed William's instructions. He moved the teaspoon slowly from side to side, and we followed it with our eyes, trying to relax all of our muscles, trying to clear our minds, concentrating on the spoon.

After a while, William set down the spoon and

stared at us expectantly. All three of us burst out laughing.

It hadn't worked.

We weren't the least bit hypnotised.

William sighed. His face fell. He was so disappointed. 'Back to the drawing board,' he muttered unhappily, shaking his head.

Of course, the jokes and wisecracks started to fly fast and furious. It would be a long time before anyone let William forget what a flop he was.

After that funny night, the four of us didn't get together again for a few weeks. I didn't see William much during that time, either.

Maybe the last night all five of us were together was the night in William's kitchen. It was a warm spring night, I remember. We were just hanging out. Marty was goofing on something or other. I think he was imitating Mr Schein, our French teacher. Erica and Stan were being sort of lovey-dovey, smooching and kidding around at the kitchen table against the wall.

Then Marty had to leave. He was late for work at the restaurant.

After he left, it got sort of quiet. William seemed to be preoccupied. He barely said a word. 'Maybe we should go, too,' Stan suggested awkwardly. He and Erica stood up from the table.

'No, wait,' William said. He glanced at me and smiled. Then he walked to the refrigerator and pulled a quart container of ice cream from the freezer.

'Hey—all right!' Stan declared. 'What flavour?'

'Heath Bar Crunch,' William replied. He took a silver ice cream scoop from the drawer and got some bowls out. I remember how the scoop seemed to glisten, catching the light from the low ceiling fixture.

The three of us stared at William as he scooped the ice cream into the bowls. I guess we were surprised that he suddenly seemed cheerful and nice, like his old self.

'Here,' William said, shoving the bowls across the counter towards us, the scoop still glistening in his hand. 'Have some ice cream.'

We started shovelling in the ice cream. It was hot in the kitchen, and it tasted really good.

But then Stan started teasing William about his hypnotism. I gave Stan a look, trying to signal to him to stop. But he didn't see me.

'Are you still into the "Look deep into my eyes" stuff?' Stan asked. 'Or have you moved on to pulling rabbits out of hats?'

Erica laughed, and, to my surprise, William chuckled, too.

Stan kept up the teasing—taking over Marty's role, I guess—begging William to show us some magic tricks, to levitate us, dumb stuff like that.

William took all the kidding good-naturedly. I hoped maybe he was returning to his old self.

Then he suggested the four of us go out for a walk. He put his arm around me as we went out the back door and headed around the house to the front. I sort of snuggled against him as we walked, feeling good about things.

It was only about nine o'clock but a lot of houses were already dark. The trees seemed to whisper in the soft, warm breeze, casting rolling shadows over the lawns.

We walked three blocks and reached Park Street. William squeezed my hand gently as a large oil truck roared past. Park Street is only two lanes. But it connects to the highway, and it is the main thoroughfare for trucks heading through town.

Several cars whirred by, and then a moving van, its enormous tyres bouncing over the bumpy pavement. Everyone seemed to ignore the speed limit on this stretch of the road. Even this late at night, Park Street was hard to cross.

'Should we head back or keep going?' Erica asked, her long black hair billowing behind her as another large truck bombed past.

William squeezed my hand again, then turned to face Erica and Stan. 'Go stand on the yellow line,' he told them, 'and don't move till I tell you.'

'William!' I exclaimed, pulling my hand free.

I expected Erica and Stan to laugh at him. But to my shock, they didn't hesitate. Without even glancing to see if anything was coming, they both stepped into the street and walked to the yellow line that ran down the middle.

'William—what are you doing?' I cried.

A car roared past, swerving to the right and blasting its horn.

Erica and Stan didn't move. They stood on the yellow line. They didn't look frightened or alarmed. Their expressions were calm.

Down the road, I saw a huge semi zooming towards them.

'William—bring them back!' I shouted. Then I started screaming at Erica and Stan. 'Come back! Get out of the street! Come back!'

The truck's horn drowned out my frantic cries. I could see the driver shaking his fist at us as he roared past without slowing.

I looked away. I couldn't bear to watch. When I turned back, Erica and Stan were still standing calmly in place in the centre of the street.

'William—please! They're going to get killed! Please!' I pleaded with him, pulling his arm.

I hated the look on his face. His grey eyes seemed to glow. His whole face was lit up by his excitement. He was so . . . happy!

'Swear to me you won't tell them what happened,' he said, leaning close, his strange eyes burning into mine.

'Huh?' I stared back at him.

'They won't remember any of it,' William said, watching with pleasure as a station wagon swerved to miss Erica and Stan. 'Swear to me you won't tell them—and I'll bring them back.'

'I swear!' I cried eagerly. I would've sworn to anything.

'Come on back!' William shouted.

Smiling pleasantly, Erica and Stan walked together across the street and rejoined us. I was so relieved, I had tears running down my cheeks.

'What's wrong, Jennifer?' Erica asked me, seeing the tears.

I glanced at William, who was watching me intently. 'The wind blew something in my eye,' I told her.

After that night, my life became something like a dream. Just bits of places and activities. A blur of faces and unconnected conversations. I'd go to school, do my homework, see my friends, talk to my parents, but everything seemed different, out of order, as if my life were a jigsaw puzzle that had been dropped on the floor, the pieces scattering everywhere.

I should have told someone—*anyone*—about what William did to Erica and Stan. But I didn't.

I can't explain why I didn't.

I really don't remember what I was thinking. My memory is so clouded.

I remember talking to Marty a few days later. School had just let out. We were standing in back near the student parking lot. The sky was solid grey, as grey as William's eyes.

I started to tell Marty that I was worried about William. He asked me why. 'He's just become so . . . weird,' I told him.

I don't know if I intended to tell Marty what William had done. Even if I had, I didn't get the chance. I suddenly realised that William was watching us. I saw him ducking down low, hiding behind the bonnet of a Honda Civic, spying on us.

I felt a cold stab of fear. 'Listen, Marty, I've got to go,' I said. Marty looked really surprised as I took off. He called after me, but I didn't stop.

William caught up with me a few blocks from my house. The sky was even darker now, and it started to drizzle. William grabbed my arm and pulled me behind the hedges of someone's yard. He looked very worked up, very angry.

'William—let go of my arm!' I cried. He was really hurting me.

He apologised but he didn't let go. 'So you're on

Marty's side, too,' he said quietly. He looked very hurt, as if I had betrayed him.

For a moment, I felt sorry for him. He was just so mixed up. I wanted to comfort him. I wanted to tell him that everything was going to be okay. I wanted to see the old William again.

But I guess that was impossible. William loosened his grip on my arm. 'There's no point in being on Marty's side,' he said softly, staring into my eyes. 'Marty is dead meat.'

'Huh? William—what on earth—?' He was scaring me now. He was really scaring me.

Why didn't I just run away? Why did I stay there and listen to him?

'Marty's going to die,' William said, his face a blank, revealing no emotion at all. 'Stan is going to do it.'

'You're kidding—right?' I managed to say. 'This is some kind of a joke?' This was too crazy. Too crazy.

'No,' he said matter-of-factly. 'Everyone is against me. Everyone is on Marty's side. I can't let that go on. You understand, Jennifer. I can't let everyone be on Marty's side. So, what can I do? What choice do I have? Stan is going to kill Marty. I'm going to hypnotise Stan and Erica. Then Stan will take his precious baseball bat and kill Marty.'

'You can't!' I managed to cry, turning my head. I suddenly couldn't bear to look at William's face. Was this the same guy I had cared so much about?

He laughed. 'Why can't I?' he demanded.

'You can't hypnotise someone to do something that's against their will. It won't work.'

His expression turned thoughtful. He was silent

for a while. My heart was pounding in my chest. The drizzle turned to rain. 'I guess you're right,' he said finally. 'I guess it won't work.'

He walked away.

I stood there for the longest time, the rain soaking my hair, soaking my clothes. I stood there watching him walk away, until he turned the corner and disappeared.

Why didn't I call the police? Or tell my parents? Or get help of any kind?

I can't explain it. My life was a dream. One scene ran into another. All a jumble.

I remember that I felt a little relieved knowing that you can't hypnotise someone and force them to do something against their will.

Knowing that made me feel a lot better.

William had even agreed with me on that.

But then I realised he had agreed much too quickly. I began to feel troubled again.

As soon as I got home, I changed into dry clothes, wrapped a towel around my wet hair, and phoned Erica. 'Listen,' I said before she could get a word in, 'William is going to try to hypnotise you and Stan.'

'Huh?' she cried. Stan must have been standing right next to her. I could hear him asking her something in the background.

'William is going to try to hypnotise you,' I repeated. 'Don't let him. Just pretend to be hypnotised, okay?'

It took me a while to persuade Erica to believe me. Finally, she started to understand. 'Let me get this straight, Jennifer. You want us to pretend to be hypnotised?'

'Yes,' I told her. 'Resist William with all your strength. You can't be hypnotised if you don't want to be. But go along with it. Afterwards, the three of us can figure out how to deal with William.'

Erica agreed and hung up to explain things to Stan.

That made me feel a little better. William's plan cannot work, I told myself. No way.

I saw him in school the next day. He smiled at me across the room during third period study hall. The smile made me feel sad. It reminded me of how William used to be.

He called me that night, an hour after dinner. 'Why don't you come over, Jennifer? Erica and Stan are already here. We're just hanging out.'

Just hanging out.

I suddenly felt cold all over. And terribly heavy, as if I were made of stone. Heavy with dread, I guess.

But I knew I had to go over to William's. I had no choice.

The three of them were in the kitchen, seated around the table when I arrived. Erica gave me a nervous glance as I came in, then quickly looked away. Stan was giggling about something with William, a high-pitched, nervous giggle I'd never heard from him before.

It was obvious to me that Erica and Stan were both terribly nervous. This hypnotism thing really had them spooked. I said hi to everyone and tossed my jacket into a corner.

William, I could see, was the only calm one in the room. He was chatting playfully with Stan, telling him something that was making Stan utter that high-pitched giggle.

'How come you called us over tonight?' Erica asked William, interrupting whatever he was telling Stan. She glanced at her watch. 'I've got a ton of homework to do. Miss Farrell really piled it on tonight.'

William stood up, smiling pleasantly at her. 'You said you were just finishing dinner when I called,' he said, walking over to the fridge. 'I thought you might like some dessert.'

He removed a quart of ice cream from the freezer, then pulled the silver ice cream scoop from the drawer and held it up so that it sparkled under the kitchen light. He opened the carton and began scooping perfect ice cream balls into the bowls.

'Here. Have some ice cream,' William said.

Then, leaving the bowls on the counter, he stepped to the head of the table and stood staring down at Stan and Erica. 'Stan, when I finish talking to you, I want you and Erica to drive to your house and get your Pete Rose bat,' he said softly, speaking slowly and distinctly.

Stan nodded in agreement.

William continued his instructions. 'Every night just after ten o'clock, Marty hauls the garbage bags out to the back entrance of the restaurant. He puts them in a Dumpster in the alley behind the restaurant. I want you two to drive to the alley. Park there. Be sure to turn off your headlights. Stan, you wait behind the Dumpster. When Marty comes out dragging the garbage bags, swing your bat at his head. I want you to hit him six times in the head. Do you understand? You swing the bat six times.'

Stan and Erica both nodded.

Erica glanced at me. Her face was as expressionless as Stan's. Neither of them reacted to William's instructions in any way. But I could tell they were faking it. I could tell they were pretending to be hypnotised.

Thank God I reached them in time, I thought. Thank God I persuaded them to resist William.

'Okay, guys. Go get the bat,' William instructed them in a low, calm voice.

Erica and Stan scooted their chairs back and climbed to their feet. Without saying a word, they headed towards the back door.

'Oh—one more thing,' William called after them. They stopped at the door and looked back. 'Stan, when you finish hitting Marty, be sure to leave the bat right next to him before you drive home.'

Stan nodded in agreement. Then he and Erica disappeared out the door.

William gave me an odd, satisfied smile, then walked to the sink and began washing off the ice cream scoop. He was humming cheerily to himself.

Too bad, William, I thought, staring hard at his back. But your hideous plan isn't going to work. Erica and Stan weren't hypnotised at all.

You're going to fail, William, I thought, standing up, picking up my jacket, preparing to leave. You're going to fail. And maybe after you fail, we can reach you again. Maybe we'll be able to help you.

He turned around. 'Where are you going?' he asked, surprised to see me putting on my jacket.

'Home,' I told him.

He shook his head. 'No. You're coming with me.'

He looked up at the brass kitchen clock over the sink. 'We're going for a ride a little later.'

I sat back down. I didn't resist.

Time passed. I don't know how much.

We were in his parents' car, driving through the night. There was a full moon and a sky full of tiny white stars. It must have been pretty late. A lot of the houses we passed were dark. There were few cars on the road.

When William turned onto Madison Drive, I realised where we were going. To the restaurant. Where Marty worked.

William turned into the alley. I squeezed the door handle, gripped by fear. I had to force myself to breathe.

In a few seconds, we'd be behind the restaurant. And William would see that his plan had failed. What would he do then? Would he figure out that I had tipped off Stan and Erica?

What would William do? What would he do to me?

The car slid slowly through the alley, brick walls on both sides of us. I squeezed the door handle and stared straight ahead through the windshield.

In the white glare of the headlights I could see the back of the restaurant now. I could see the kitchen door, half open, a thin rectangle of grey fluorescent light, escaping from inside.

I could see two metal trash cans lying on their sides, their lids beside them in the concrete alley. I could see a large green Dumpster. I could see a plastic garbage bag on the ground in front of the Dumpster, full, on its side, open, some of its contents having spilled to the ground.

And then the headlights seemed to focus on the body lying in front of the toppled garbage bag. It was Marty. Sprawled face down in a round, dark puddle of blood. His arms and legs stretched out on the pavement. His head bashed in, still oozing blood. The baseball bat lying at his feet.

'No! No—no—no!'

Was that *me* screaming?

Something snapped. My mind suddenly felt so clear. As if a weight had been lifted. As if a heavy curtain had been pulled away.

'No—no—no!!'

Yes, it *was* me screaming.

And now I was pushing open the car door, running hard, my sneakers thudding on the hard alley concrete, gasping for breath. I was running away. I was escaping from William.

I was free. Finally free.

Everything was so clear.

Without slowing down, I glanced back. William wasn't coming after me. The car hadn't moved. He was still behind the wheel.

I was free. I was getting away.

I ran all the way home. It didn't take long. I knew what I had to do. I had to call the police.

Finally, I could call the police. Finally, I could get help.

I burst through the front door, calling my mom and dad. But no one was home. I stopped in the front hallway, leaned against the banister, rested my head on the railing. I waited for the throbbing in my temples to stop, waiting for my breathing to return to normal.

Then I walked across the dark living room to the phone in the corner next to the couch. As I reached for the receiver, the phone rang.

A chill ran down my back. 'Hello?'

'Hi, Jennifer. It's me.' William.

'William—I have to talk to you,' I said, unable to hide the fear in my voice.

'It's too late for talking,' he replied calmly. 'I have to come over now, Jennifer. I have to . . . deal with you.'

'But, William—'

'I took care of Marty,' he said, his voice low and steady. 'I took care of Stan and Erica because they were on Marty's side. Now you're the only one left.'

'But I don't understand,' I cried, gripping the phone so hard my hand ached. 'You *couldn't* have hypnotised them. I *told* them to resist. I told them just to pretend.'

I could hear him chuckle on the other end of the line. It was the most frightening sound I had ever heard. 'I didn't need to hypnotise them,' he explained. 'They were already hypnotised, Jennifer. I hypnotised all three of you that day at the Pizza Palace.'

'No, you didn't!' I cried. 'You failed—remember?'

'I made you think I failed.'

'But, William, how—?'

'Jennifer, haven't you ever heard of a posthypnotic suggestion? I hypnotised you at the pizza restaurant. I gave you all a posthypnotic suggestion. So there was never any need to hypnotise you again.'

'But, William—'

'No more talking,' he said abruptly. 'I have no

choice. I have to take care of you, too, Jennifer. I'm coming right over.'

I realised I was trembling all over, trembling so hard, I nearly dropped the phone. 'William—?'

The line was silent for a moment. And then William said, 'Here. Have some ice cream.'

He hung up right after that.

And I'm sitting here in the dark in front of the phone.

I know I should call the police. Or run. Or *something.*

But I don't seem to be able to.

It's so dark in here. So quiet.

Oh, well. William will be here any minute.

Maybe he'll tell me what to do.

*   *   *

R.L. STINE is the author of the *Goosebumps, Fear Street* ('Where your worst nightmares live!') and *Ghosts of Fear Street* series which are the biggest-selling paperbacks for young readers in the world. He has been called the number one children's author of all time and his books 'the live action *X Files* for kids'. It has been reckoned that he has sold over 300 million books—and that was just at the last count! His spooky stories have also been adapted for TV in the *Goosebumps* series in which boys and girls get the better of each other—and adults, too—in all manner of frightening ways.

Robert Lawrence Stine was born in Columbus, Ohio, and started writing stories and joke books when he was nine. He says he loved the old horror comics

like *Vault of Horror* which were always available to read
at his local hairdressers—so he would get his hair
cut every week and now jokes, 'I had no hair at all
when I was a kid!' His first job was as a junior high
school teacher, and when he later moved to New
York he started writing tales of adventure and funny
stories for children under the name of 'Jovial Bob'.
But his love of old horror movies—especially *Creature
from the Black Lagoon*—encouraged him to try his
hand at a scary story and his first book, *Blind Date*
(nothing to do with the TV series), was an immediate
best-seller.

According to R.L. Stine everything in his books is
true. 'It actually happened to me,' he says. 'You can't
imagine what a *horrifying* life I've led—but at least
I've been able to get a few books out of it!' He has
a teenage son, Matt, and says he loves the letters he
gets from readers all over the world. 'I received one
from a boy who, while he was reading one of my
books, started screaming so loud his parents came
running to see what was the matter. That made me
feel really proud!' Is he ever scared? 'I don't even
dare have nightmares,' he says. 'My dreams are very
boring, too. Once I dreamt about making a sausage
sandwich. Now *that's* scary!'

IT'S A GOOD LIFE

Jerome Bixby

Anthony, like William in the last story, has weird supernatural powers, but he's had them since birth. He can make birds drop out of the sky, cause insects to fly straight into spiders' webs, and even get rats to believe they can smell cheese and run into his traps. When he's not around, people refer to him as 'a nice, nice Goblin', but warn their kids not to go too near because he can read minds. If Anthony likes someone, he'll use his powers to help them; but if he doesn't, then some very scary things indeed can happen.

*   *   *

Aunt Amy was out on the front porch, rocking back and forth in the highbacked chair and fanning herself, when Bill Soames rode his bicycle up the road and stopped in front of the house.

Perspiring under the afternoon sun, Bill lifted the box of groceries out of the big basket over the front wheel of the bike, and came up the front walk.

Little Anthony was sitting on the lawn, playing with a rat. He had caught the rat down in the basement—he had made it think that it smelled cheese, the most rich-smelling and crumbly-delicious cheese a rat had ever thought it smelled, and it had come out of its hole and now Anthony had hold of it with his mind and was making it do tricks.

When the rat saw Bill Soames coming, it tried to run, but Anthony thought at it, and it turned a flip-flop on the grass and lay trembling, its eyes gleaming in small black terror.

Bill Soames hurried past Anthony and reached the front steps, mumbling. He always mumbled when he came to the Fremont house, or passed it by, or even thought of it. Everybody did. They thought about silly things, things that didn't mean very much, like two-and-two-is-four-and-twice-is-eight and so on; they tried to jumble up their thoughts and keep them skipping back and forth, so Anthony couldn't read their minds. The mumbling helped. Because if Anthony got anything strong out of your thought, he might take a notion to do something about it—like curing your wife's sick headaches or your kid's mumps, or getting your old milk cow back on schedule, or fixing the privy. And while Anthony mightn't actually mean any harm, he couldn't be expected to have much notion of what was the right thing to do in such cases.

That was if he liked you. He might try to help you, in his way. And that could be pretty horrible.

If he didn't like you . . . well, that could be worse.

Bill Soames set the box of groceries on the porch railing, and stopped his mumbling long enough to say, 'Everythin' you wanted, Miss Amy.'

'Oh, fine, William,' Amy Fremont said lightly. 'My ain't it terrible hot today?'

Bill Soames almost cringed. His eyes pleaded with her. He shook his head violently *no*, and then interrupted his mumbling again, though obviously he didn't want to: 'Oh, don't say that, Miss Amy . . . it's fine, just fine. A real *good* day!'

Amy Fremont got up from the rocking chair, and came across the porch. She was a tall woman, thin, a smiling vacancy in her eyes. About a year ago, Anthony had gotten mad at her, because she'd told him he shouldn't have turned the cat into a cat-rug, and although he had always obeyed her more than anyone else, which was hardly at all, this time he'd snapped at her. With his mind. And that had been the end of Amy Fremont's bright eyes, and the end of Amy Fremont as everyone had known her. And that was when word got around in Peaksville (population: 46) that even the members of Anthony's own family weren't safe. After that, everyone was twice as careful.

Some day Anthony might undo what he'd done to Aunt Amy. Anthony's Mom and Pop hoped he would. When he was older, and maybe sorry. If it was possible, that is. Because Aunt Amy had changed a lot, and besides, now Anthony wouldn't obey anyone.

'Land alive, William,' Aunt Amy said, 'you don't have to mumble like that. Anthony wouldn't hurt you. My goodness, Anthony likes you!' She raised her voice and called to Anthony, who had tired of the rat and was making it eat itself. 'Don't you, dear? Don't you like Mr Soames?'

Anthony looked across the lawn at the grocery man—a bright, wet, purple gaze. He didn't say anything. Bill Soames tried to smile at him. After a second Anthony returned his attention to the rat. It had already devoured its tail, or at least chewed it off—for Anthony had made it bite faster than it could swallow, and little pink and red furry pieces lay around it on the green grass. Now the rat was having trouble reaching its hindquarters.

Mumbling silently, thinking of nothing in particular as hard as he could, Bill Soames went stiff-legged down the walk, mounted his bicycle and pedalled off.

'We'll see you tonight, William,' Aunt Amy called after him.

As Bill Soames pumped the pedals, he was wishing deep down that he could pump twice as fast, to get away from Anthony all the faster, and away from Aunt Amy, who sometimes just forgot how *careful* you had to be. And he shouldn't have thought that. Because Anthony caught it. He caught the desire to get away from the Fremont house as if it was something *bad*, and his purple gaze blinked, and he snapped a small, sulky thought after Bill Soames—just a small one, because he was in a good mood today, and besides, he liked Bill Soames, or at least didn't dislike him, at least today. Bill Soames wanted to go away—so, petulantly, Anthony helped him.

Pedalling with superhuman speed—or rather, appearing to, because in reality the bicycle was pedalling *him*—Bill Soames vanished down the road in a cloud of dust, his thin, terrified wail drifting back across the summerlike heat.

Anthony looked at the rat. It had devoured half its belly, and had died from pain. He thought it into a grave out deep in the cornfield—his father had once said, smiling, that he might as well do that with the things he killed—and went around the house, casting his odd shadow in the hot, brassy light from above.

*

In the kitchen, Aunt Amy was unpacking the groceries. She put the Mason-jarred goods on the shelves, and the meat and milk in the icebox, and the beet sugar and coarse flour in big cans under the sink. She put the cardboard box in the corner, by the door, for Mr Soames to pick up next time he came. It was stained and battered and torn and worn fuzzy, but it was one of the few left in Peaksville. In faded red letters it said *Campbell's Soup*. The last cans of soup, or of anything else, had been eaten long ago, except for a small communal hoard which the villagers dipped into for special occasions—but the box lingered on, like a coffin, and when it and the other boxes were gone, the men would have to make some out of wood.

Aunt Amy went out in back, where Anthony's Mom—Aunt Amy's sister—sat in the shade of the house, shelling peas. The peas, every time Mom ran a finger along a pod, went *lollop-lollop-lollop* into the pan on her lap.

'William brought the groceries,' Aunt Amy said. She sat down wearily in the straight-backed chair beside Mom, and began fanning herself again. She wasn't really old; but ever since Anthony had snapped at her with his mind, something had seemed to be wrong with her body as well as her mind, and she was tired all the time.

'Oh, good,' said Mom. *Lollop* went the fat peas into the pan.

Everybody in Peaksville always said 'Oh fine,' or 'Good,' or 'Say, that's swell!' when almost anything happened or was mentioned—even unhappy things like accidents or even deaths. They'd always say

'Good,' because if they didn't try to cover up how they really felt, Anthony might overhear with his mind and then nobody knew what might happen. Like the time Mrs Kent's husband, Sam, had come walking back from the graveyard, because Anthony liked Mrs Kent and had heard her mourning.

Lollop.

'Tonight's television night,' said Aunt Amy. 'I'm glad. I look forward to it so much every week. I wonder what we'll see tonight?'

'Did Bill bring back the meat?' asked Mom.

'Yes.' Aunt Amy fanned herself, looking up at the featureless brassy glare of the sky. 'Goodness, it's hot! I wish Anthony would make it just a little cooler—'

'*Amy!*'

'Oh!' Mom's sharp tone had penetrated, where Bill Soames' agonised expression had failed. Aunt Amy put one thin hand to her mouth in exaggerated alarm. 'Oh ... I'm sorry, dear.' Her pale blue eyes shuttled around, right and left, to see if Anthony was in sight. Not that it would make any difference if he was or wasn't—he didn't have to be near you to know what you were thinking. Usually, though, unless he had his attention on somebody, he would be occupied with thoughts of his own.

But some things attracted his attention—you could never be sure just what.

'This weather's just *fine*,' Mom said.

Lollop.

'Oh, yes,' Aunt Amy said. 'It's a wonderful day. I wouldn't want it changed for the world!'

Lollop.

Lollop.

'What time is it?' Mom asked.

Aunt Amy was sitting where she could see through the kitchen window to the alarm clock on the shelf above the stove. 'Four-thirty,' she said.

Lollop.

'I want tonight to be something special,' Mom said. 'Did Bill bring a good lean roast?'

'Good and lean, dear. They butchered just today, you know, and sent us over the best piece.'

'Dan Hollis will be *so* surprised when he finds out that tonight's television party is a birthday party for him too!'

'Oh *I* think he will! Are you sure nobody's told him?'

'Everybody swore they wouldn't.'

'That'll be real nice,' Aunt Amy nodded, looking off across the cornfield. 'A birthday party.'

'Well—' Mom put the pan of peas down beside her, stood up and brushed her apron. 'I'd better get the roast on. Then we can set the table.' She picked up the peas.

Anthony came around the corner of the house. He didn't look at them, but continued on down through the carefully kept garden—*all* the gardens in Peaksville were carefully kept, very carefully kept—and went past the rusting, useless hulk that had been the Fremont family car, and went smoothly over the fence and out into the cornfield.

'Isn't this a lovely day!' said Mom, a little loudly, as they went towards the back door.

Aunt Amy fanned herself. 'A beautiful day, dear. Just *fine!*'

*

Out in the cornfield, Anthony walked between the tall, rustling rows of green stalks. He liked to smell the corn. The alive corn overhead, and the old dead corn underfoot. Rich Ohio earth, thick with weeds and brown, dry-rotting ears of corn, pressed between his bare toes with every step—he had made it rain last night so everything would smell and feel nice today.

He walked clear to the edge of the cornfield, and over to where a grove of shadowy green trees covered cool, moist, dark ground and lots of leafy undergrowth and jumbled moss-covered rocks and a small spring that made a clear, clean pool. Here Anthony liked to rest and watch the birds and insects and small animals that rustled and scampered and chirped about. He liked to lie on the cool ground and look up through the moving greenness overhead, and watch the insects flit in the hazy soft sunbeams that stood like slanting, glowing bars between ground and treetops. Somehow, he liked the thoughts of the little creatures in this place better than the thoughts outside; and while the thoughts he picked up here weren't very strong or very clear, he could get enough out of them to know what the little creatures liked and wanted, and he spent a lot of time making the grove more like what they wanted it to be. The spring hadn't always been here; but one time he had found thirst in one small furry mind, and had brought subterranean water to the surface in a clear cold flow, and had watched blinking as the creature drank, feeling its pleasure. Later he had made the pool, when he found a small urge to swim.

He had made rocks and trees and bushes and caves,

and sunlight here and shadows there, because he had felt in all the tiny minds around him the desire—or the instinctive want—for this kind of resting place, and that kind of mating place, and this kind of place to play, and that kind of home.

And somehow the creatures from all the fields and pastures around the grove had seemed to know that this was a good place, for there were always more of them coming in—every time Anthony came out here there were more creatures than the last time, and more desires and needs to be tended to. Every time there would be some kind of creature he had never seen before, and he would find its mind, and see what it wanted, and then give it to it.

He liked to help them. He liked to feel their simple gratification.

Today, he rested beneath a thick elm, and lifted his purple gaze to a red and black bird that had just come to the grove. It twittered on a branch over his head, and hopped back and forth, and thought its tiny thoughts, and Anthony made a big, soft nest for it, and pretty soon it hopped in.

A long, brown, sleek-furred animal was drinking at the pool. Anthony found its mind next. The animal was thinking about a smaller creature that was scurrying along the ground on the other side of the pool, grubbing for insects. The little creature didn't know that it was in danger. The long, brown animal finished drinking and tensed its legs to leap, and Anthony thought it into a grave in the cornfield.

He didn't like those kind of thoughts. They reminded him of the thoughts outside the grove. A long time ago some of the people outside had thought that way about *him*, and one night they'd hidden and waited for him to come back from the grove—and he'd just thought them all into the cornfield. Since then, the rest of the people hadn't thought that way—at least, very clearly. Now their thoughts were all mixed up and confusing whenever they thought about him or near him, so he didn't pay much attention.

He liked to help them, too, sometimes—but it wasn't simple, or very gratifying either. They never thought happy thoughts when he did—just the jumble. So he spent more time out here.

He watched all the birds and insects and furry creatures for a while, and played with a bird, making it soar and dip and streak madly around tree trunks until, accidentally, when another bird caught his attention for a moment, he ran it into a rock. Petulantly, he thought the rock into a grave in the cornfield; but he couldn't do anything more with the bird. Not because it was dead, though it was; but because it had a broken wing. So he went back to the house. He didn't feel like walking back through the cornfield, so he just *went* to the house, right down into the basement.

It was nice down here. Nice and dark and damp and sort of fragrant, because once Mom had been making preserves in a rack along the far wall and then she'd stopped coming down ever since Anthony had started spending time here, and the preserves had spoiled and leaked down and spread over the dirt floor, and Anthony liked the smell.

He caught another rat, making it smell cheese, and

after he played with it, he thought it into a grave right beside the long animal he'd killed in the grove. Aunt Amy hated rats, and so he killed a lot of them, because he liked Aunt Amy most of all and sometimes did things that Aunt Amy wanted. Her mind was more like the little furry minds out in the grove. She hadn't thought anything bad at all about him for a long time.

After the rat, he played with a big black spider in the corner under the stairs, making it run back and forth until its web shook and shimmered in the light from the cellar window like a reflection in silvery water. Then he drove fruit flies into the web until the spider was frantic trying to wind them all up. The spider liked flies, and its thoughts were stronger than theirs, so he did it. There was something bad in the way it liked flies, but it wasn't clear—and besides, Aunt Amy hated flies too.

He heard footsteps overhead—Mom moving around in the kitchen. He blinked his purple gaze, and almost decided to make her hold still—but instead he went up to the attic, and, after looking out of the circular window for a while at the front lawn and the dusty road and Henderson's tip-waving wheatfield beyond, he curled into an unlikely shape and went partly to sleep.

Soon people would be coming for television, he heard Mom think.

He went more to sleep. He liked television night. Aunt Amy had always liked television a lot, so one time he had thought some for her, and a few other people had been there at the time, and Aunt Amy had felt disappointed when they wanted to leave.

He'd done something to them for that—and now everybody came to television.

He liked all the attention he got when they did.

Anthony's father came home around six-thirty, looking tired and dirty and bloody. He'd been over in Dunn's pasture with the other men, helping pick out the cow to be slaughtered this month and doing the job, and then butchering the meat and salting it away in Soames's icehouse. Not a job he cared for, but every man had his turn. Yesterday, he had helped scythe down old McIntyre's wheat. Tomorrow, they would start threshing. By hand. Everything in Peaksville had to be done by hand.

He kissed his wife on the cheek and sat down at the kitchen table. He smiled and said, 'Where's Anthony?'

'Around someplace,' Mom said.

Aunt Amy was over at the wood-burning stove, stirring the big pot of peas. Mom went back to the oven and opened it and basted the roast.

'Well, it's been a *good* day,' Dad said. By rote. Then he looked at the mixing bowl and breadboard on the table. He sniffed at the dough. 'M'm,' he said. 'I could eat a loaf all by myself, I'm so hungry.'

'No one told Dan Hollis about it being a birthday party, did they?' his wife asked.

'Nope. We kept as quiet as mummies.'

'We've fixed up such a lovely surprise!'

'Um? What?'

'Well . . . you know how much Dan likes music. Well, last week Thelma Dunn found a *record* in her attic!'

'No!'

'Yes! And we had Ethel sort of ask—you know, without really *asking*—if he had that one. And he said no. Isn't that a wonderful surprise?'

'Well, now, it sure is. A record, imagine! That's a real nice thing to find! What record is it?'

'Perry Como, singing *You Are My Sunshine.*'

'Well, I'll be darned. I always liked that tune.' Some raw carrots were lying on the table. Dad picked up a small one, scrubbed it on his chest, and took a bite. 'How did Thelma happen to find it?'

'Oh, you know—just looking around for new things.'

'M'm.' Dad chewed the carrot. 'Say, who has that picture we found a while back? I kind of liked it— that old clipper sailing along—'

'The Smiths. Next week the Sipichs get it and they give the Smiths old McIntyre's music box, and we give the Sipichs—' And she went down the tentative order of things that would exchange hands among the women at church this Sunday.

He nodded, 'Looks like we can't have the picture for a while, I guess. Look, honey, you might try to get that detective book back from the Reillys. I was so busy the week we had it, I never got to finish all the stories.'

'I'll try,' his wife said doubtfully. 'But I hear the van Husens have a stereoscope they found in the cellar.' Her voice was just a little accusing. 'They had it two whole months before they told anybody about it—'

'Say,' Dad said, looking interested. 'That'd be nice, too. Lots of pictures?'

'I suppose so. I'll see on Sunday. I'd like to have it—but we still owe the van Husens for their canary. I don't know why that bird had to pick *our* house to die . . . it must have been sick when we got it. Now there's just no satisfying Betty van Husen—she even hinted she'd like our *piano* for a while!'

'Well, honey, you try for the stereoscope—or just anything you think we'll like.' At last he swallowed the carrot. It had been a little young and tough. Anthony's whims about the weather made it so that people never knew what crops would come up, or what shape they'd be in if they did. All they could do was plant a lot; and always enough of something came up any one season to live on. Just once there had been a grain surplus; tons of it had been hauled to the edge of Peaksville and dumped off into the nothingness. Otherwise, nobody could have breathed when it started to spoil.

'You know,' Dad went on. 'It's nice to have the new things around. It's nice to think that there's probably still a lot of stuff nobody's found yet, in cellars and attics and barns and down behind things. They help, somehow. As much as anything can help—'

'Sh-h!' Mom glanced nervously around.

'Oh,' Dad said smiling hastily. 'It's all right! The new things are *good*! It's *nice* to be able to have something around you've never seen before, and know that something you've given somebody else is making them happy . . . that's a real *good* thing.'

'A good thing,' his wife echoed.

'Pretty soon,' Aunt Amy said, from the stove, 'there won't be any more new things. We'll have found everything there is to find. Goodness, that'll be too bad—'

'*Amy!*'

'Well—' Her pale eyes were shallow and fixed, a sign of her recurrent vagueness. 'It will be kind of a shame—no new things—'

'Don't *talk* like that,' Mom said, trembling. 'Amy, be *quiet!*'

'It's *good*,' said Dad, in the loud, familiar, wanting-to-be-overheard tone of voice. 'Such talk is *good*. It's okay, honey—don't you see? It's good for Amy to talk any way she wants. It's good for her to feel bad. Everything's good. Everything *has* to be good . . .'

Anthony's mother was pale. And so was Aunt Amy—the peril of the moment had suddenly penetrated the clouds surrounding her mind. Sometimes it was difficult to handle words so that they might not prove disastrous. You just never *knew*. There were so many things it was wise not to say, or even think— but remonstration for saying or thinking them might be just as bad, if Anthony heard and decided to do anything about it. You could just never tell what Anthony was liable to do.

Everything had to be good. Had to be fine just as it was, even if it wasn't. Always. Because any change might be worse. So terribly much worse.

'Oh, my goodness, yes, of course it's good,' Mom said. 'You talk any way you want to, Amy, and it's just fine. Of course, you want to remember that some ways are *better* than others . . .'

Aunt Amy stirred the peas, fright in her pale eyes.

'Oh, yes,' she said. 'But I don't feel like talking right now. It . . . it's *good* that I don't feel like talking.'

Dad said tiredly, smiling, 'I'm going out and wash up.'

They started arriving around eight o'clock. By that time, Mom and Aunt Amy had the big table in the dining-room set, and two more tables off to the side. The candles were burning, and the chairs situated, and Dad had a big fire going in the fireplace.

The first to arrive were the Sipichs, John and Mary. John wore his best suit, and was well scrubbed and pink-faced after his day in McIntyre's pasture. The suit was neatly pressed, but getting threadbare at elbows and cuffs. Old McIntyre was working on a loom, designing it out of schoolbooks, but so far it was slow going. McIntyre was a capable man with wood and tools, but a loom was a big order when you couldn't get metal parts. McIntyre had been one of the ones who, at first, had wanted to try to get Anthony to make things the villagers needed, like clothes and canned goods and medical supplies and gasoline. Since then, he felt that what had happened to the whole Terrance family and Joe Kinney was his fault, and he worked hard trying to make it up to the rest of them. And since then, no one had tried to get Anthony to do anything.

Mary Sipich was a small, cheerful woman in a simple dress. She immediately set about helping Mom and Aunt Amy put the finishing touches on the dinner.

The next arrivals were the Smiths and Dunns, who lived right next to each other down the road, only a few yards from the nothingness. They drove up in the Smiths' wagon, drawn by their old horse.

Then the Reillys showed up, from across the darkened wheatfield, and the evening really began. Pat Reilly sat down at the big upright in the front room, and began to play from the popular sheet music on the rack. He played softly, as expressively as he could—and nobody sang. Anthony liked piano playing a whole lot, but not singing; often he would come up from the basement, or down from the attic, or just *come*, and sit on top of the piano, nodding his head as Pat played *Lover* or *Boulevard of Broken Dreams* or *Night and Day*. He seemed to prefer ballads, sweetsounding songs—but the one time somebody had started to sing, Anthony had looked over from the top of the piano and done something that made everybody afraid of singing from then on. Later they'd decided that the piano was what Anthony had heard first, before anybody had ever tried to sing, and now anything else added to it didn't sound right and distracted him from his pleasure.

So, every television night, Pat would play the piano, and that was the beginning of the evening. Wherever Anthony was, the music would make him happy, and put him in a good mood, and he would know that they were gathering for television and waiting for him.

By eight-thirty everybody had shown up, except for the seventeen children and Mrs Soames who was off watching them in the schoolhouse at the far end of town. The children of Peaksville were never, never allowed near the Fremont house—not since little Fred Smith had tried to play with Anthony on a dare. The younger children weren't even told about Anthony. The others had mostly forgotten about him,

or were told that he was a nice, nice goblin but they
must never go near him.

Dan and Ethel Hollis came late, and Dan walked
in not suspecting a thing. Pat Reilly had played the
piano until his hands ached—he'd worked pretty
hard with them today—and now he got up, and everybody gathered around to wish Dan Hollis a happy
birthday.

'Well, I'll be darned,' Dan grinned. 'This is
swell, I wasn't expecting this at all . . . gosh, this is
swell!'

They gave him his presents—mostly things they
had made by hand, though some were things that
people had possessed as their own and now gave
him as his. John Sipich gave him a watch charm,
hand-carved out of a piece of hickory wood. Dan's
watch had broken down a year or so ago, and there
was nobody in the village who knew how to fix it, but
he still carried it around because it had been his
grandfather's and was a fine old heavy thing of gold
and silver. He attached the charm to the chain, while
everybody laughed and said John had done a nice
job of carving. Then Mary Sipich gave him a knitted
necktie, which he put on, removing the one he'd
worn.

The Reillys gave him a little box they had made,
to keep things in. They didn't say what things, but
Dan said he'd keep his personal jewellery in it. The
Reillys had made it out of a cigar box, carefully peeled
of its paper and lined on the inside with velvet. The
outside had been polished, and carefully if not
expertly carved by Pat—but his carving got complimented too. Dan Hollis received many other gifts—

a pipe, a pair of shoelaces, a tie pin, a knitted pair of socks, some fudge, a pair of garters made from old suspenders.

He unwrapped each gift with vast pleasure, and wore as many of them as he could right there, even the garters. He lit up the pipe, and said he'd never had a better smoke, which wasn't quite true, because the pipe wasn't broken in yet. Pete Manners had had it lying around ever since he'd received it as a gift four years ago from an out-of-town relative who hadn't known he'd stopped smoking.

Dan put the tobacco into the bowl very carefully. Tobacco was precious. It was only pure luck that Pat Reilly had decided to try to grow some in his backyard just before what had happened to Peaksville had happened. It didn't grow very well, and then they had to cure it and shred it and all, and it was just precious stuff. Everybody in town used wooden holders old McIntyre had made, to save on butts.

Last of all, Thelma Dunn gave Dan Hollis the record she had found.

Dan's eyes misted even before he opened the package. He knew it was a record.

'Gosh,' he said softly. 'What one is it? I'm almost afraid to look . . .'

'You haven't got it, darling,' Ethel Hollis smiled. 'Don't you remember, I asked about *You Are My Sunshine?*'

'Oh, gosh,' Dan said again. Carefully he removed the wrapping and stood there fondling the record, running his big hands over the worn grooves with their tiny, dulling crosswise scratches. He looked

around the room, eyes shining, and they all smiled
back, knowing how delighted he was.

'Happy birthday, darling!' Ethel said, throwing her
arms around him and kissing him.

He clutched the record in both hands, holding it
off to one side as she pressed against him. 'Hey,' he
laughed, pulling back his head. 'Be careful ... I'm
holding a priceless object!' He looked around again,
over his wife's arms, which were still around his neck.
His eyes were hungry. 'Look ... do you think we
could play it? Lord, what I'd give to hear some new
music ... just the first part, the orchestra part, before
Como sings?'

Faces sobered. After a minute, John Sipich said, 'I
don't think we'd better, Dan. After all, we don't know
just where the singer comes in—it'd be taking too
much of a chance. Better wait till you get home.'

Dan Hollis reluctantly put the record on the buffet
with all his other presents. 'It's *good*,' he said automatically, but disappointedly, 'that I can't play it
here.'

'Oh, yes,' said Sipich. 'It's good.' To compensate
for Dan's disappointed tone, he repeated, 'It's
good.'

They ate dinner, the candles lighting their smiling
faces, and ate it all right down to the last delicious
drop of gravy. They complimented Mom and Aunt
Amy on the roast beef, and the peas and carrots, and
the tender corn on the cob. The corn hadn't come
from the Fremonts' cornfield, naturally—everybody
knew what was out there, and the field was going to
weeds.

Then they polished off the dessert—homemade ice cream and cookies. And then they sat back, in the flickering light of the candles, and chatted, waiting for television.

There never was a lot of mumbling on television night—everybody came and had a good dinner at the Fremonts', and that was nice, and afterwards there was television, and nobody really thought much about that—it just had to be put up with. So it was a pleasant enough get-together, aside from your having to watch what you said just as carefully as you always did everywhere. If a dangerous thought came into your mind, you just started mumbling, even right in the middle of a sentence. When you did that, the others just ignored you until you felt happier again and stopped.

Anthony liked television night. He had done only two or three awful things on television night in the whole past year.

Mom had put a bottle of brandy on the table, and they each had a tiny glass of it. Liquor was even more precious than tobacco. The villagers could make wine, but the grapes weren't right, and certainly the techniques weren't, and it wasn't very good wine. There were only a few bottles of real liquor left in the village—four rye, three Scotch, three brandy, nine real wine and half a bottle of Drambuie belonging to old McIntyre (only for marriages)—and when those were gone, that was it.

Afterwards, everybody wished that the brandy hadn't been brought out. Because Dan Hollis drank more of it than he should have, and mixed it with a lot of the homemade wine. Nobody thought anything about it at first, because he didn't show it much out-side, and it was his birthday party and a happy party, and Anthony liked these get-togethers and shouldn't see any reason to do anything even if he was listening.

But Dan Hollis got high, and did a fool thing. If they'd seen it coming, they'd have taken him outside and walked him around.

The first thing they knew, Dan stopped laughing right in the middle of the story about how Thelma Dunn had found the Perry Como record and dropped it and it hadn't broken because she'd moved faster than she ever had before in her life and caught it. He was fondling the record again, and looking longingly at the Fremonts' gramophone over in the corner, and suddenly he stopped laughing and his face got slack, and then it got ugly, and he said, 'Oh, *Christ!*'

Immediately the room was still. So still they could hear the whirring movement of the grandfather's clock out in the hall. Pat Reilly had been playing the piano, softly. He stopped, his hands poised over the yellowed keys.

The candles on the dining-room flickered in a cool breeze that blew through the lace curtains over the bay window.

'Keep playing, Pat,' Anthony's father said softly.

Pat started again. He played *Night and Day*, but his eyes were sidewise on Dan Hollis, and he missed notes.

Dan stood in the middle of the room, holding the record. In his other hand he held a glass of brandy so hard his hand shook.

They were all looking at him.

'*Christ,*' he said again, and made it sound like a dirty word.

Reverend Younger, who had been talking with Mom and Aunt Amy by the dining-room door, said 'Christ' too—but he was using it in a prayer. His hands were clasped, and his eyes were closed.

John Sipich moved forward. 'Now, Dan . . . it's *good* for you to talk that way. But you don't want to talk too much, you know?'

Dan shook off the hand Sipich put on his arm.

'Can't even play my record,' he said loudly. He looked down at the record, and then around at their faces. 'Oh, my *God* . . .'

He threw the glassful of brandy against the wall. It splattered and ran down the wallpaper in streaks.

Some of the women gasped.

'Dan,' Sipich said in a whisper. 'Dan, cut it out—'

Pat Reilly was playing *Night and Day* louder, to cover up the sounds of the talk. It wouldn't do any good, though, if Anthony was listening.

Dan Hollis went over to the piano and stood by Pat's shoulder, swaying a little.

'Pat,' he said. 'Don't play *that*. Play *this*.' And he began to sing. Softly, hoarsely, miserably: 'Happy birthday to me . . . Happy birthday to me . . .'

'*Dan!*' Ethel Hollis screamed. She tried to run across the room to him. Mary Sipich grabbed her arm and held her back. 'Dan,' Ethel screamed again. 'Stop—'

'My God, be quiet!' hissed Mary Sipich, and pushed her towards one of the men, who put his hand over her mouth and held her still.

'—Happy Birthday, dear Danny,' Dan sang. 'Happy birthday to me!' He stopped and looked down at Pat Reilly. 'Play it, Pat. Play it, so I can sing right . . . you know I can't carry a tune unless somebody plays it!'

Pat Reilly put his hands on the keys and began *Lover*—in a low waltz tempo, the way Anthony liked it. Pat's face was white. His hands fumbled.

Dan Hollis stared over at the dining-room door. At Anthony's mother, and at Anthony's father who had gone to join her.

'You had him,' he said. Tears gleamed on his cheeks as the candlelight caught them. '*You* had to go and *have* him . . .'

He closed his eyes, and the tears squeezed out. He sang loudly, 'You are my sunshine . . . my only sunshine . . . you make me happy . . . when I am blue . . .'

Anthony came into the room.

Pat stopped playing. He froze. Everybody froze. The breeze rippled the curtains. Ethel Hollis couldn't even try to scream—she had fainted.

'Please don't take my sunshine . . . away . . . Dan's voice faltered into silence. His eyes widened. He put both hands out in front of him, the empty glass in one, the record in the other. He hiccupped, and said, '*No*—'

'Bad man,' Anthony said, and thought Dan Hollis into something like nothing anyone would have believed possible, and then he thought the thing into a grave deep, deep in the cornfield.

The glass and record thumped on the rug. Neither broke.

Anthony's purple gaze went around the room.

Some of the people began mumbling. They all tried to smile. The sound of mumbling filled the room like a far-off approval. Out of the murmuring came one or two clear voices:

'Oh, it's a very *good* thing,' said John Sipich.

'A good thing,' said Anthony's father, smiling. He'd had more practice in smiling that most of them. 'A wonderful thing.'

'It's swell . . . just swell,' said Pat Reilly, tears leaking from eyes and nose, and he began to play the piano again, softly, his trembling hands feeling for *Night and Day*.

Anthony climbed up on top of the piano, and Pat played for two hours.

Afterwards, they watched television. They all went into the front room, and lit just a few candles, and pulled up chairs around the set. It was a small-screen set, and they couldn't all sit close enough to it to see, but that didn't matter. They didn't even turn the set on. It wouldn't have worked anyway, there being no electricity in Peaksville.

They just sat silently, and watched the twisting, writhing shapes on the screen, and listened to the sounds that came out of the speaker, and none of them had any idea of what it was all about. They never did. It was always the same.

'It's real nice,' Aunty Amy said once, her pale eyes on the meaningless flickers and shadows. 'But I liked it a little better when there were cities outside and we could get real—'

'Why, Amy!' said Mom. 'It's good for you to say such a thing. Very good. But how can you mean it?

Why, this television is *much* better than anything we ever used to get!'

'Yes,' chimed in John Sipich. 'It's fine. It's the best show we've ever seen!'

He sat on the couch, with two other men, holding Ethel Hollis flat against the cushions, holding her arms and legs and putting their hands over her mouth, so she couldn't start screaming again.

'It's really *good!*' he said again.

Mom looked out of the front window, across the darkened road, across Henderson's darkened wheat field to the vast, endless, grey nothingness in which the little village of Peaksville floated like a soul— the huge nothingness that was most evident at night, when Anthony's brassy day had gone.

It did no good to wonder where they were . . . no good at all. Peaksville was just somewhere. Somewhere away from the world. It was wherever it had been since that day three years ago when Anthony had crept from her womb and old Doc Bates—God rest him—had screamed and dropped him and tried to kill him, and Anthony had whined and done the thing. Had taken the village somewhere. Or had destroyed the world and left only the village, nobody knew which.

It did no good to wonder about it. Nothing at all did any good—except to live as they must live. Must always, always live, if Anthony would let them.

These thoughts were dangerous, she thought.

She began to mumble. The others started mumbling too. They had all been thinking, evidently.

The men on the couch whispered and whispered to Ethel Hollis and when they took their hands away, she mumbled too.

While Anthony sat on top of the set and made television, they sat around and mumbled and watched the meaningless, flickering shapes far into the night.

Next day it snowed, and killed off half the crops— but it was a *good* day.

*   *   *

JEROME BIXBY wrote this great story back in 1953 when I was a teenager, and as much as any other weird tale it turned me on to horror stories. It has influenced a lot of other writers since, including several who have contributed to this book and consider it to be a classic. Bixby has written lots of other creepy short stories as well as the screenplay for a famous horror movie, *It! The Terror from Beyond Space* and several *Star Trek* episodes and novelisations. 'It's a Good Life' has twice been adapted for the screen: originally in 1961 for the *Twilight Zone* television series with Billy Mumy playing Anthony Fremont, and in *Twilight Zone: The Movie,* when Jeremy Licht starred as the tyrant kid with superpowers and a grown-up Billy Mumy (then 29) made a cameo appearance as one of his victims. The screenplay was written by Richard Matheson whose own story comes next . . .

DRINK MY RED BLOOD

Richard Matheson

Jules is a pale, delicate little boy who hates sunlight. As a baby, his first spoken word was 'Death', and as he grew up he spent a lot of his time on his own making up spooky words like 'nighttouch' and 'killove'. Most other children have grown wary of him and his face makes a lot of adults shiver whenever he walks by. Then one night at the cinema, the strange little boy sees Dracula. *The film does not scare him—far from it. Now Jules wants to be a vampire himself . . .*

*   *   *

The people on the block decided definitely that Jules was crazy when they heard about his composition.

There had been suspicions for a long time.

He made people shiver with his blank stare. His coarse guttural tongue sounded unnatural in his frail body. The paleness of his skin upset many children. It seemed to hang loose around his flesh. He hated sunlight.

And his ideas were a little out of place for the people who lived on the block.

Jules wanted to be a vampire.

People declared it common knowledge that he was born on a night when winds uprooted trees. They said he was born with three teeth. They said he'd used them to fasten himself on his mother's breast, drawing blood with the milk.

They said he used to cackle and bark in his crib after dark. They said he walked at two months and sat staring at the moon whenever it shone.

Those were things that people said.

His parents were always worried about him. An only child, they noticed his flaws quickly.

They thought he was blind until the doctor told them it was just a vacuous stare. He told them that Jules, with his large head, might be a genius or an idiot. It turned out he was an idiot.

He never spoke a word until he was five. Then one night coming up to supper, he sat down at the table and said, 'Death.'

His parents were torn between delight and disgust. They finally settled for a place in between the two feelings. They decided that Jules couldn't have realised what the word meant.

But Jules did.

From that night on, he built up such a large vocabulary that everyone who knew him was astonished. He not only acquired every word spoken to him, words from signs, magazines, books; he made up his own words.

Like nighttouch. Or killove. They were really several words that melted into each other. They said things Jules felt but couldn't explain with other words.

He used to sit on the porch while the other children played hopscotch, stickball and other games. He sat there and stared at the sidewalk and made up words.

Until he was twelve Jules kept pretty much out of

trouble. Of course there was the time they found him undressing Olive Jones in an alley. And another time he was discovered dissecting a kitten on his bed.

But there were many years in between. Those scandals were forgotten.

In general he went through childhood merely disgusting people.

He went to school but never studied. He spent about two or three terms in each grade. The teachers all knew him by his first name. In some subjects like reading and writing he was almost brilliant.

In others he was hopeless.

One Saturday when he was twelve, Jules went to the movies. He saw *Dracula*.

When the show was over he walked, a throbbing nerve mass, through the little girl and boy ranks.

He went home and locked himself in the bathroom for two hours.

His parents pounded on the door and threatened but he wouldn't come out.

Finally he unlocked the door and sat down at the supper table. He had a bandage on his thumb and a satisfied look on his face.

The morning after he went to the library. It was Sunday. He sat on the steps all day waiting for it to open. Finally he went home.

The next morning he came back instead of going to school.

He found *Dracula* on the shelves. He couldn't borrow it because he wasn't a member and to be a member he had to bring in one of his parents.

So he stuck the book down his pants and left the library and never brought it back.

He went to the park and sat down and read the book through. It was late evening before he finished.

He started at the beginning again, reading as he ran from street light to street light, all the way home.

He didn't hear a word of the scolding he got for missing lunch and supper. He ate, went to his room and read the book to the finish. They asked him where he got the book. He said he found it.

As the days passed Jules read the story over and over. He never went to school.

Late at night, when he had fallen into an exhausted slumber, his mother used to take the book into the living-room and show it to her husband.

One night they noticed that Jules had underlined certain sentences with dark shaky pencil lines.

Like: 'The lips were crimson with fresh blood and the stream had trickled over her chin and stained the purity of her lawn death robe.'

Or: 'When the blood began to spurt out, he took my hands in one of his, holding them tight and, with the other seized my neck and pressed my mouth to the wound . . .'

When his mother saw this, she threw the book down the garbage chute.

The next morning when Jules found the book missing he screamed and twisted his mother's arm until she told him where the book was.

Then he ran down to the cellar and dug in the piles of garbage until he found the book.

Coffee grounds and egg yolk on his hands and wrists, he went to the park and read it again.

For a month he read the book avidly. Then he

knew it so well he threw it away and just thought about it.

Absence notes were coming from school. His mother yelled. Jules decided to go back for a while. He wanted to write a composition.

One day he wrote it in class. When everyone was finished writing, the teacher asked if anyone wanted to read their compositions to the class.

Jules raised his hand.

The teacher was surprised. But she felt charity. She wanted to encourage him. She drew in her tiny jab of a chin and smiled.

'All right,' she said, 'pay attention, children. Jules is going to read us his composition.'

Jules stood up. He was excited. The paper shook in his hands.

'My Ambition by . . .'

'Come to the front of the class, Jules, dear.'

Jules went to the front of the class. The teacher smiled lovingly. Jules started again.

'My Ambition by Jules Dracula.'

The smile sagged.

'When I grow up I want to be a vampire.'

The teacher's smiling lips jerked down and out. Her eyes popped wide.

'I want to live forever and get even with everybody and make all the girls vampires. I want to smell of death.'

'Jules!'

'I want to have a foul breath that stinks of dead earth and crypts and sweet coffins.'

The teacher shuddered. Her hands twitched on her green blotter. She couldn't believe her ears. She looked at the children. They were gaping. Some of them were giggling. But not the girls.

'I want to be all cold and have rotten flesh with stolen blood in the veins.'

'That will . . . hrrumph!'

The teacher cleared her throat mightily.

'That will be all, Jules,' she said.

Jules talked louder and desperately.

'I want to sink my terrible white teeth in my victims' necks. I want them to . . .'

'Jules! Go to your seat this instant!'

'I want them to slide like razors in the flesh and into the veins,' read Jules ferociously.

The teacher jolted to her feet. Children were shivering. None of them were giggling.

'Then I want to draw my teeth out and let the blood flow easy in my mouth and run hot in my throat and . . .'

The teacher grabbed his arm. Jules tore away and ran to a corner. Barricaded behind a stool he yelled:

'And drip off my tongue and run out of my lips down my victim's throats! I want to drink girls' blood!'

The teacher lunged for him. She dragged him out of the corner. He clawed at her and screamed all the way to door and the principal's office.

'That is my ambition! That is my ambition! That is my ambition!'

It was grim.

Jules was locked in his room. The teacher and the principal sat with Jules' parents. They were talking in sepulchral voices.

They were recounting the scene.

All along the block parents were discussing it. Most of them didn't believe it at first. They thought their children made it up.

Then they thought what horrible children they'd raised if the children could make up such things.

So they believed it.

After that everyone watched Jules like a hawk. People avoided his touch and look. Parents pulled their children off the street when he approached. Everyone whispered tales of him.

There were more absence notes.

Jules told his mother he wasn't going to school any more. Nothing would change his mind. He never went again.

When a truant officer came to the apartment Jules would run over the roofs until he was far away from there.

A year wasted by.

Jules wandered the streets searching for something; he didn't know what. He looked in alleys. He looked in garbage cans. He looked in lots. He looked on the east side and the west side and in the middle.

He couldn't find what he wanted.

He rarely slept. He never spoke. He stared down all the time. He forgot his special words.

Then.

One day in the park, Jules strolled through the zoo.

An electric shock passed through him when he saw the vampire bat.

His eyes grew wide and his discoloured teeth shone dully in a wide smile.

From that day on, Jules went daily to the zoo and looked at the bat. He spoke to it and called it the

Count. He felt in his heart it was really a man who had changed.

A rebirth of culture struck him.

He stole another book from the library. It told all about wildlife.

He found the page on the vampire bat. He tore it out and threw the book away.

He learned the section by heart.

He knew how the bat made its wound. How it lapped up the blood like a kitten drinking cream. How it walked on folded wing stalks and hind legs like a black furry spider. Why it took no nourishment but blood.

Month after month Jules stared at the bat and talked to it. It became the one comfort in his life. The one symbol of dreams come true.

One day Jules noticed that the bottom of the wire covering the cage had come loose.

He looked around, his back eyes shifting. He didn't see anyone looking. It was a cloudy day. Not many people were there.

Jules tugged at the wire.

It moved a little.

Then he saw a man come out of the monkey house. So he pulled back his hand and strolled away whistling a song he had just made up.

Late at night, when he was supposed to be asleep, he would walk barefoot past his parents' room. He would hear his rather and mother snoring. He would hurry out, put on his shoes and run to the zoo.

Every time the watchman was not around, Jules would tug at the wiring.

He kept on pulling it loose.

When he had finished and had to run home, he pushed the wire in again. Then no one could tell.

All day Jules would stand in front of the cage and look at the Count and chuckle and tell him he'd soon be free again.

He told the Count all the things he knew. He told the Count he was going to practise climbing down walls head first.

He told the Count not to worry. He'd soon be out. Then, together, they could go all around and drink girls' blood.

One night Jules pulled the wire out and crawled under it into the cage.

It was very dark.

He crept on his knees to the little wooden house. He listened to see if he could hear the Count squeaking.

He stuck his arm in the black doorway. He kept whispering.

He jumped when he felt a needle jab in his finger.

With a look of great pleasure on his thin face, Jules drew the fluttering hairy bat to him.

He climbed down from the cage with it and ran out of the zoo; out of the park. He ran down the silent streets.

It was getting late in the morning. Light touched the dark skies with grey. He couldn't go home. He had to have a place.

He went down an alley and climbed over a fence. He held tight to the bat. It lapped at the dribble of blood from his finger.

He went across a yard and into a little deserted shack.

It was dark inside and damp. It was full of rubble and tin cans and soggy cardboard and excrement.

Jules made sure there was no way the bat could escape.

Then he pulled the door tight and put a stick through the metal loop.

He felt his heart beating hard and his limbs trembling.

He let go of the bat. It flew to a dark corner and hung on the wood.

Jules feverishly tore off his shirt. His lips shook. He smiled a crazy smile.

He reached down into his pants pocket and took out a little penknife he had stolen from his mother.

He opened it and ran a finger over the blade. It sliced through the flesh.

With shaking fingers he jabbed at his throat. He hacked. The blood ran through his fingers.

'Count! Count!' he cried in frenzied joy. 'Drink my red blood! Drink me! Drink me!'

He stumbled over the tin cans and slipped and felt for the bat. It sprang from the wood and soared across the shack and fastened itself on the other side.

Tears ran down Jules' cheeks.

He gritted his teeth. The blood ran across his shoulders and across his thin, hairless chest.

His body shook in fever. He staggered back towards the other side. He tripped and felt his side torn open on the sharp edge of a tin can.

His hands went out. They clutched the bat. He

placed it against his throat. He sank on his back on the cool wet earth. He sighed.

He started to moan and clutch at his chest. His stomach heaved. The black bat on his neck silently lapped his blood.

Jules felt his life seeping away.

He thought of all the years past. The waiting. His parents. School. Dracula. Dreams. For this. This sudden glory.

Jules' eyes flickered open.

The side of the reeking shack swam about him.

It was hard to breathe. He opened his mouth to gasp in the air. He sucked it in. It was foul. It made him cough. His skinny body lurched on the cold ground.

Mists crept away in his brain.

One by one like drawn veils.

Suddenly his mind was filled with terrible clarity.

He knew he was lying half-naked on garbage and letting a flying bat drink his blood.

With a strangled cry, he reached up and tore away the furry throbbing bat. He flung it away from him. It came back fanning his face with its vibrating wings.

Jules staggered to his feet.

He felt for the door. He could hardly see. He tried to stop his throat from bleeding so.

He managed to get the door open.

Then, lurching into the dark yard, he fell on his face in the long grass blades.

He tried to call out for help.

But no sounds save a bubbling mockery of words came from his lips.

He heard the fluttering wings.

Then, suddenly they were gone.

Strong fingers lifted him gently.Through dying eyes Jules saw the tall dark man whose eyes shone like rubies.

'My son,' the man said.

*　　*　　*

RICHARD MATHESON is an American novelist and screenwriter who has been called one of the most significant modern creators of terror and fantasy in books and on film—and the story you have read shows why. He began writing when he was nine, in the *Brooklyn Eagle*, and sold his first short story, 'Born of Man and Woman', in 1950 while he was still at college. This scary tale of an imprisoned mutant child plotting revenge on his parents gave him instant notoriety, but he became a best-seller with *I Am Legend*, about a world overrun by vampires, which was later filmed and is also the inspiration for the George A. Romero film *The Night of the Living Dead.* Richard Matheson has written a number of scripts for cinema versions of tales by the classic horror story author, Edgar Allan Poe, including *The Fall of the House of Usher* and *The Pit and the Pendulum,* and has contributed episodes to popular TV series such as *Star Trek.* Recently he has begun collaborating on stories with his son, Richard Christian Matheson, who is one of the highly-regarded new wave of sf and horror writers.

SOMETHING NASTY

William F. Nolan

Janey hates it when Uncle Gus comes visiting. It's not just that he tells her off for making too much noise or won't let her play with the cat, Whiskers, because it bothers him, it's also the way her mother always gets herself looking so nice *when he arrives. It makes no difference to Janey that her mum says Uncle Gus adores her: she* knows *he likes to upset her, to frighten her—especially with the spooky stories he tells her whenever no one else is around. But should she believe him when he tells her the scariest tale of all—that there is something really nasty living* inside *her stomach?*

*   *   *

'Have you had your shower yet, Janey?'

Her mother's voice from below stairs, drifting smokily up to her, barely audible where she lay in her bed.

Louder now; insistent. 'Janey! Will you *answer* me!'

She got up, cat-stretched, walked into the hall, to the landing, where her mother could hear her. 'I've been reading.'

'But I *told* you that Uncle Gus was coming over this afternoon.'

'I hate him,' said Janey softly.

'You're muttering. I can't understand you.' Frustration. Anger and frustration. 'Come down here at once.' When Janey reached the bottom of the stairs her mother's image was rippled. The little girl blinked rapidly, trying to clear her watering eyes.

Janey's mother stood tall and ample-fleshed and fresh-smelling above her in a satiny summer dress.

Mommy always looks nice when Uncle Gus is coming.

'Why are you crying?' Anger had given way to concern.

'Because,' said Janey.

'Because why?'

'Because I don't want to talk to Uncle Gus.'

'But he *adores* you! He comes over especially to see you.'

'No, he doesn't,' said Janey, scrubbing at her cheek with a small fist. 'He doesn't adore me and he doesn't come specially to see me. He comes to get money from Daddy.'

Her mother was shocked. 'That's a terrible thing to say!'

'But it's true. *Isn't* it true?'

'Your Uncle Gus was hurt in the war. He can't hold down an ordinary job. We just do what we can to help him.'

'He never liked me,' said Janey. 'He says I make too much noise. And he never lets me play with Whiskers when he's here.'

'That's because cats bother him. He's not used to them. He doesn't like furry things.' Her mother touched at Janey's hair. Soft gold. 'Remember that mouse you got last Christmas, how nervous it made him . . . Remember?'

'Pete was smart,' said Janey. 'He didn't like Uncle Gus, same as me.'

'Mice neither like nor dislike people,' Janey's mother told her. 'They're not intelligent enough for that.'

Janey shook her head stubbornly. 'Pete was *very* intelligent. He could find cheese anywhere in my room, no matter where I hid it.'

'That has to do with a basic sense of smell, not intelligence,' her mother said. 'But we're wasting time here, Janey. You run upstairs, take your shower and then put on your pretty new dress. The one with red polka dots.'

'They're strawberries. It has little red strawberries on it.'

'Fine. Now just do as I say. Gus will be here soon and I want my brother to be *proud* of his niece.'

Blonde head down, her small heels dragging at the top of each step, Janey went back upstairs.

'I'm not going to report this to your father,' Janey's mother was saying, her voice dimming as the little girl continued upward. 'I'll just tell him you overslept.'

'I don't care what you tell Daddy,' murmured Janey. The words were smothered in hallway distance as she moved towards her room.

Daddy would believe anything Mommy told him. He always did. Sometimes it was true, about over-sleeping. It was hard to wake up from her afternoon nap. *Because I put off going to sleep. Because I hate it.* Along with eating broccoli, and taking coloured vita-min pills in little animal shapes and seeing the dentist and going on roller coasters.

Uncle Gus had taken her on a high, scary roller

coaster ride last summer at the park, and it had made her vomit. He liked to upset her, frighten her. Mommy didn't know about all the times Uncle Gus said scary things to her, or played mean tricks on her, or took her places she didn't want to go. Mommy would leave her with him while she went shopping, and Janey absolutely *hated* being there in his dark old house. He knew the dark frightened her. He'd sit there in front of her with all the lights out, telling spooky stories, with sick, awful things in them, his voice oily and horrible. She'd get so scared, listening to him, that sometimes she'd cry.

And that made him smile.

'Gus. Always so *good* to see you!'

'Hi, Sis.'

'C'mon inside. Jim's puttering around out back somewhere. I've fixed us a nice lunch. Sliced turkey. And I made some cornbread.'

'So where's my favourite niece?'

'Janey's due down here any second. She'll be wearing her new dress—just for you.'

'Well, now, isn't that nice.'

She was watching from the top of the stairs, lying flat on her stomach so she wouldn't be seen. It made her sick, watching Mommy hug Uncle Gus that way, each time he came over, as if he had been *years* between visits. Why couldn't Mommy see how mean Uncle Gus was? All of her friends in class saw he was a bad person the first day he took her to school. Kids can tell right away about a person. Like that mean ole Mr Kruger in geography, who made Janey stay after class when she forgot to do her homework. All the kids knew that Mr Kruger was *awful.* Why does it take grown-ups so long to know things?

Janey slid backwards into the hall shadows. Stood up. Time to go downstairs. In her playclothes. Probably meant she'd get a spanking after Uncle Gus left, but it would be worth it not to have to put on her new dress for him. Spankings don't hurt *too* much. Worth it.

'Well, *here's* my little princess!' Uncle Gus was lifting her hard into the air, to make her dizzy. He knew how much she hated being swung around in the air. He set her down with a thump. Looked at her with his big cruel eyes. 'And where's that pretty new dress your Mommy told me about?'

'It got torn,' Janey said, staring at the carpet. 'I can't wear it today.'

Her mother was angry again. 'That is *not* true, young lady, and you know it! I ironed that dress this morning and it is perfect.' She pointed upwards. 'You march right back upstairs to your room and put on that dress!'

'No, Maggie.' Gus shook his head. 'Let the child stay as she is. She looks fine. Let's just have lunch.' He prodded Janey in the stomach. 'Bet that little tummy of yours is starved for some turkey.'

And Uncle Gus pretended to laugh. Janey was never fooled; she knew real laughs from pretend laughs. But Mommy and Daddy never seemed to know the difference.

Janey's mother sighed and smiled at Gus. 'All right, I'll let it go this time—but I really think you spoil her.'

'Nonsense. Janey and I understand each other.'
He stared down at her. 'Don't we, sweetie?'

Lunch was no fun. Janey couldn't finish her mashed
potatoes, and she'd just nibbled at her turkey. She
could never enjoy eating with her uncle there. As
usual, her father barely noticed she was at the table.
He didn't care if she wore her new dress or not.
Mommy took care of her and Daddy took care of
business, whatever that was. Janey could never figure
out what he did, but he left every day for some office
she'd never seen and he made enough money there
so that he always had some to give to Uncle Gus when
Mommy asked him for a cheque.

Today was Sunday so Daddy was home with his big
newspaper to read and the car to wax and the grass
to trim. He did the same things every Sunday.

*Does Daddy love me? I know that Mommy does, even
though she spanks me sometimes. But she always hugs me
after. Daddy never hugs me. He buys me ice cream, and he
takes me to the movies on Saturday afternoon, but I don't
think he loves me.*

Which is why she could never tell him the truth
about Uncle Gus. He'd never listen.

And Mommy just didn't understand.

After lunch, Uncle Gus grabbed Janey firmly by the
hand and took her into the back yard. Then he sat
her down next to him on the big wooden swing.

'I'll bet your new dress is *ugly*,' he said in a cold voice.

'Is not. It's pretty!'

Her discomfort pleased him. He leaned over, close
to her right ear. 'Want to know a secret?'

Janey shook her head. 'I want to go back with Mommy. I don't like being out here.'

She started away, but he grabbed her, pulling her roughly back onto the swing. 'You *listen* to me when I talk to you.' His eyes glittered. 'I'm going to tell you a secret. About yourself.'

'Then tell me.'

He grinned. 'You've got something inside.'

'What's that mean?'

'It means there's something deep down inside your rotten little belly. And it's *alive!*'

'Huh?' She blinked, beginning to get scared.

'A creature. That lives off what you eat and breathes the air you breathe and can see out of your eyes.' He pulled her face close to his. 'Open your mouth, Janey, so I can look in and see what's living down there!'

'No, I *won't.*' She attempted to twist away, but he was too strong. 'You're lying! You're just telling me an awful *lie!* You *are!*'

'Open wide.' And he applied pressure to her jaw with the fingers of his right hand. Her mouth opened. 'Ah, that's better. Let's have a look . . .' He peered into her mouth. 'Yes, *there.* I can see it now.'

She drew back, eyes wide, really alarmed. 'What's it like?'

'Nasty! Horrid. With very sharp teeth. A *rat*, I'd say. Or something *like* a rat. Long and grey and plump.'

'I don't have it! I *don't!*'

'Oh, but you do, Janey.' His voice was oily. 'I saw its red eyes shining and its long snaky tail. It's down there all right. Something nasty.'

And he laughed. Real, this time. No pretend laugh. Uncle Gus was having himself some fun.

Janey knew he was just trying to scare her again—but she wasn't absolutely one hundred per cent sure about the thing inside. Maybe he *had* seen something.

'Do ... any other people have ... creatures ... living in them?'

'Depends,' said Uncle Gus. 'Bad things live inside bad people. Nice little girls don't have them.'

'I'm nice!'

'Well now, that's a matter of opinion, isn't it?' His voice was soft and unpleasant. 'If you *were* nice, you wouldn't have something nasty living inside.'

'I don't believe you,' said Janey, breathing fast. 'How could it be real?'

'Things are real when people believe in them.' He lit a long black cigarette, drew in the smoke, exhaled it slowly. 'Have you ever heard of voodoo, Janey?'

She shook her head.

'The way it works it—this witch doctor puts a curse on someone by making a doll and sticking a needle into the doll's heart. Then he leaves the doll at the house of the man he's cursed. When the man sees it he becomes very frightened. He makes the curse real by *believing* in it.'

'And then what happened?'

'His heart stops and he dies.'

Janey felt her own heart beating very rapidly.

'You're afraid, aren't you, Janey?'

'Maybe ... a little.'

'You're afraid, all right.' He chuckled. 'And you should be—with a thing like that inside you!'

'You're a very bad and wicked man!' she told him, tears misting her eyes.

And she ran swiftly back to the house.

That night, in her room, Janey sat rigid in bed, hugging Whiskers. He liked to come in late after dark and curl up on the coverlet just under her feet and snooze there until dawn. He was an easy-going, grey-and-black housecat who never complained about anything and always delivered a small 'meep' of contentment whenever Janey picked him up for some stroking. Then he would begin to purr.

Tonight Whiskers was not purring. He sensed the harsh vibrations in the room, sensed how upset Janey was. He quivered uneasily in her arms.

'Uncle Gus lied to me, didn't he, Whiskers?' The little girl's voice was strained, uncertain. 'See . . .' She hugged the cat closer. 'Nothing's down there, huh?'

And she yawned her mouth wide to show her friend that no rat-thing lived there. If one did, ole Whiskers would be sticking a paw inside to get it. But the cat didn't react. Just blinked slitted green eyes at her.

'I knew it,' Janey said, vastly relieved. 'If I just don't believe it's in there, then it *isn't.*'

She slowly relaxed her tensed body muscles—and Whiskers, sensing a change, began to purr—a tiny, soothing motorised sound in the night.

Everything was all right now. No red-eyed creature existed in her tummy. Suddenly she felt exhausted. It was late, and she had school tomorrow.

Janey slid down under the covers and closed her

eyes, releasing Whiskers, who padded to his usual spot on the bed.

She had a lot to tell her friends.

It was Thursday, a day Janey usually hated. Every other Thursday her mother went shopping and left her to have lunch with Uncle Gus in his big spooky house with the shutters closed tight against the sun and shadows filling every hallway.

But *this* Thursday would be all different, so Janey didn't mind when her mother drove off and left her alone with her uncle. *This* time, she told herself, she wouldn't be afraid. A giggle.

She might even have fun!

When Uncle Gus put Janey's soup plate in front of her he asked her how she was feeling.

'Fine,' said Janey quietly, eyes down.

'Then you'll be able to appreciate the soup.' He smiled, trying to look pleasant. 'It's a special recipe. Try it.'

She spooned some into her mouth.

'How does it taste?'

'Kinda sour.'

Gus shook his head, trying some for himself. 'Ummm . . . delicious.' He paused. 'Know what's in it?'

She shook her head.

He grinned, leaning towards her across the table. 'It's owl-eye soup. Made from the dead eyes of an owl. All mashed up fresh, just for you.'

She looked at him steadily. 'You want me to upchuck, don't you, Uncle Gus?'

'My goodness no, Janey.' There was oiled delight in his voice. 'I just thought you'd like to know what you swallowed.'

Janey pushed her plate away. 'I'm not going to be sick because I don't believe you. And when you don't believe in something then it's not real.'

Gus scowled at her, finishing his soup.

Janey knew he planned to tell her another awful spook story after lunch, but she wasn't upset about that. Because.

Because there wouldn't *be* any after lunch for Uncle Gus.

It was time for her surprise.

'I got something to tell you, Uncle Gus.'

'So tell me.' His voice was sharp and ugly.

'All my friends at school know about the thing inside. We talked about it a lot and now we all believe in it. It has red eyes and it's furry and it smells bad. And it's got lots of very sharp teeth.'

'You *bet* it has,' Gus said, brightening at her words. 'And it's always hungry.'

'But guess what,' said Janey. 'Surprise! It's not inside me, Uncle Gus . . . it's inside *you!*'

He glared at her. 'That's not funny, you little bitch. Don't try to turn this around and pretend that—'

He stopped in mid-sentence, spoon clattering to the floor as he stood up abruptly. His face was flushed. He made strangling sounds.

'It wants out,' said Janey.

Gus doubled over the table, hands clawing at his stomach. 'Call . . . call a . . . doctor!' he gasped.

'A doctor won't help,' said Janey in satisfaction. 'Nothing can stop it now.'

Janey followed him calmly, munching on an apple. She watched him stagger and fall in the doorway, rolling over on his back, eyes wild with panic.

She stood over him, looking down at her uncle's stomach under the white shirt.

Something *bulged* there.

Gus screamed.

Late that night, alone in her room, Janey held Whiskers tight against her chest and whispered into her pet's quivering ear. 'Mommy's been crying,' she told the cat. 'She's real upset about what happened to Uncle Gus. Are *you* upset, Whiskers?'

The cat yawned, revealing sharp white teeth.

'I didn't think so. That's because you didn't like Uncle Gus any more than me, did you?'

She hugged him. 'Wanta hear a *secret*, Whiskers?'

The cat blinked lazily at her, beginning to purr.

'You know that mean ole Mr Kruger at school . . . well, guess what?' She smiled. 'Me an' the other kids are gonna talk to him tomorrow about something he's got inside him.' Janey shuddered deliciously. 'Something nasty!'

And she giggled.

*　　*　　*

WILLIAM F. NOLAN once drove racing cars and was a commercial artist before launching his career in America as a successful novelist, short story writer and film and television scriptwriter. He became famous with his story *Logan's Run*, about a world of the future where young people have taken over and everyone is killed when they reach the age of 21. It was filmed in 1976 and then adapted as a television series. He has written a number of short stories in which children get their revenge on cruel adults, but none more scary than 'Something Nasty' which he says is based on a real person. 'I had an uncle who really bugged me when I was growing up,' he explains. 'Every time he came to our house on a visit he'd tell me to "Hush, boy!" or "Be Quiet!" or "Quit jumping around!" I never felt I was being noisy, but *he* obviously did. As a result of this constant badgering, I began to resent his visits, much to my mother's distress, since she dearly loved her brother. Many decades later, my fictional "Uncle Gus" was born in the pages of this story—of course, he's *much* nastier than my real uncle!'

THE RESTLESS GHOST

Leon Garfield

Dick Bostock and his friend Harris are planning to frighten the miserable, bad-tempered old sexton who works at the church said to be haunted by the ghost of a smugglers' drummer boy that glows *in the darkness. But when Dick dresses up as the ghost, in clothes specially covered in phosphorescent paint—an eerie mixture of pigments—and begins to beat on an old drum, he very soon finds himself coming face to face with something far more scary than an old man who has a hatred of mischievous small boys . . .*

*   *   *

D'you know the old church at Hove—the ruined one that lies three-quarters of a mile back from the sea and lets the moon through like a church of black Nottingham lace?

Not an agreeable place, with its tumbledown churchyard brooded over by twelve elms and four threadbare yews which seemed to be in mourning for better weather. A real disgrace to the Christian dead.

Twice a month the vicar used to preach briefly; then be glad to get back to Preston. For he, no more than anyone, like the villainous old crow of a sexton.

A mean, shrivelled, horny, sour, fist-shaking and

shouting old man was the sexton, a hater of most things, but particularly boys.

Some said the reason for his ill-temper was a grumbling belly; others said it was bunions (on account of his queer bounding limp when chasing off marauders and young hooters among his tombs); and others muttered that he was plagued by a ghost.

D'you remember the ghost? It was a drummer boy who used to drift through the churchyard on misty Saturday nights, glowing blue and green and drumming softly—to the unspeakable terror of all.

But that was twenty years ago. Then, two years after the haunting had begun, a certain band of smugglers had been caught and hanged—every last one of them in a dismal, dancing line—but not before they'd made a weird confession. They said the ghostly drummer had been no worse than a foundling lad, smeared with phosphorous to glow and gleam and scare off interruption while the smugglers followed darkly on. For the churchyard had been their secret pathway to the safety of the Downs and beyond.

But that was eighteen years ago. The foundling lad had vanished and the smugglers had all mouldered away. So why was the old sexton such a misery and so violent against idly mischievous boys? What had they ever done to him (save hoot and squeak among his graves), so that he should rush out and threaten them with his spade and an old musket that was no more use than a rotten branch?

An interesting question; and one that absorbed two pupils of Dr Barron's school in Brighthelmstone to the exclusion of their proper studies. Their names? Dick Bostock and his dear friend, R. Harris.

'What say we scare the dying daylights out of him on Saturday night?' said Bostock to Harris on the Wednesday before it.

Harris, who was a physician's son and therefore interested in all things natural and supernatural, nodded his large head. Harris was thirteen and somewhat the more intellectual; but Bostock, though younger by a year, was the more widely profound. Even separately, they were of consequence, but together they were of sombre ingenuity and frantic daring.

So it was that, during three long and twilight walks to their separate homes, they hit on a singularly eerie scheme.

And all the while, in his cottage by the lych-gate, brooded the savage old sexton, unknowing that his angry days were numbered; and that two formidable pupils of Dr Barron's had cast up their score.

'I'll give him something to moan about!' said Bostock, deeply.

'That you will,' agreed Harris, with a gloomy admiration ... for his part in the strange scheme was limited to fetching its wherewithal.

They met for the final time on the Saturday afternoon—as the light was dying—in an obscure lane two hundred yards to the north of the church.

They met in silence, as became their enterprise; but with nods and smiles, as became the success of it.

They walked for a little way till they came to a break in the hedge that led to a spot of some secrecy. There they unburdened themselves of their bundles.

'On a misty Saturday night...' murmured Bostock, drawing out of his bundle a scarlet and black striped coat.

'. . . There walked among the graves,' whispered Harris, producing an old grenadier's cap.

'A fearful, ghostly drummer boy,' said Bostock, bringing forth the necessary drum that rattled softly as he laid it in the long, still grass. He paused, then added:

'Glowing?'

'Blue and green,' nodded Harris, holding up a small stone pot, stolen from his father's laboratory.

In this was the phosphorescent paint—an eerie mixture of yellow phosphates and pigmented ointment—furtively compounded by Harris from the recipe he had copied out of the condemned smuggler's confession.

The clothes they had borrowed off a brandy merchant whose son had gone for a soldier and not come back—were exactly as the smugglers had declared. ('We dressed him as a grenadier, yer Honour. 'Twas all we had to hand.')

Hurriedly—for the day was almost gone—Dick Bostock put the garments on. As he did so, he felt a strange, martial urge quicken his heart and run through his veins.

He took the drum, slung it about his neck—and could scarcely prevent himself from rolling and rattling upon it then and there.

Instead of which, watched by the silent Harris, he marched stiffly up and down as if possessed by the spirits of all the valorous youths who'd ever gone to war. Indeed, so brightly gleamed his eyes, that he might well have done without the ghostly paint; but

Harris, whose masterpiece it was, now offered it with a trembling hand.

'Now the sea mist's come, it'll not be dangerous,' he murmured, shivering slightly as a heavy damp came drifting through the hedge.

'Dangerous?' said Bostock scornfully.

'Moistness is necessary,' said Harris, stroking the pot. 'It takes fire or burns in dry air. But the mists will keep it damp . . .' Then, clutched with a sudden uneasiness, he muttered urgently: 'Bostock! don't be overlong.'

'Come, Harris! Open it up! Paint me, Harris. Make me glow and gleam. I'll be but half an hour in the churchyard. More than enough to frighten that dismal pig out of his wits. Then I'll be back with you safe and sound. I'll not outstay the mists—I promise you! Don't shake and shiver, Harris! D'you think I am to stand among the tombs till I take fire and frizzle like a sausage?'

Harris continued to shiver; but even so, his more cautious soul was shamed before Bostock's valour . . . which appeared even more striking by reason of the grenadier's cap and drum.

He opened the pot. And from it, as if there had been something within that had been sleeping—a monstrous glow-worm, maybe—there came slowly forth a pale, evil gleaming . . .

Little by little, this uncanny light increased, shedding its queer radiance on the boys' peering faces—and beyond them to the dense hawthorns that clustered about, touching the tips of the twigs with the bright buds of a Devil's Spring.

'Paint me, Harris,' breathed Bostock.

So Harris, with a spatula stolen from his father's dispensary, began to smear the weird ointment on to the drummer's coat, his cuffs, his grenadier's cap, the front of his breeches, the tarnished cords of his drum, the drumsticks, and—

'My face, Harris. Dab some on my face!'

'No, not there, Bostock! Not your face! There may be danger from it...'

'Then my hands, Harris. You must paint my hands!'

Once more, Harris was overcome. With the spatula that shook so much that the evil substance spattered the grass with its chilly gleaming, he scraped a thin layer on the young skin of Bostock's hands.

To Bostock the ointment felt unnaturally cold—even piercingly so. The heavy chill of it seemed to sink into the bones of his fingers and from thence to creep upward...

With a scowl of contempt at his own imagining, he seized up the shining drumsticks—and brought them down on the drum with a sharp and formidable sound. Then again ... and again, till the sticks quivered on the stretched skin as if in memory of the ominous rattle of war. And he began to stalk to and fro...

Harris fell back, transfixed with a terrified admiration. Glowing green and blue, with bony rattle and a shadowy smile, there marched the ghostly drummer to the very mockery of life.

'Am I fearful?' whispered Bostock, stopping the drumming and overcome with awe at the terror in his companion's eyes.

'Horrible, Bostock. Did I not know it was you, I'd drop down stone dead with fright.'

'Do I walk like a ghost?' pursued Bostock.

Harris, who'd never viewed a ghost, considered it would need a pretty remarkable spectre to come even within moaning distance of the grim and ghastly Bostock. He nodded.

'Then let's be gone,' said Bostock, as hollowly as he might. 'Watch from a distance, Harris. See without being seen.'

Again, Harris nodded. Whereupon the phosphorescent drummer stalked eerily off, drumming as he went, towards the silent church.

The sea mists were now visiting among the elms of the churchyard, sometimes drifting out like bulky grey widows, for to peer at the inscription on some tumbled altar-tomb, before billowing off as in search of another, dearer one . . .

The light from the sexton's cottage glimmered fitfully among the branches of one of the yews—for all the world as if the angry old man had at last given up human company and made his home in that dark, tangled place.

Bostock, watched by fascinated Harris from the churchyard's edge—smiled deeply, and stalked on.

Drum . . . drum . . . drum! the battalions are coming! From where? From the mists and the shuddering tombs . . . platoons of long dead grenadiers pricked up their bony heads at the call of the old drum; grinned—nodded—moved to arms . . .

Or so it seemed to the phosphorescent Bostock as he trundled back and forth, uneasily enjoying himself and awaiting the sexton's terror.

Now the sound of his drum seemed to echo—

doubtless by reason of the confining mists. He must remember to ask Harris about it. Harris knew of such things. (Also the banking vapours seemed to reflect back, here and there, his own phosphorescence, as if in a foul mirror.)

Sea mists were queer; especially at night. But he was grateful that their heavy damp eased the tingling on his hands. The ointment was indeed a powerful one.

There was no sign yet of the sexton. Was it possible he hadn't heard the drum? Could the horrible old man have gone deaf? With a touch of irritation, Bostock began to drum more loudly, and stalked among the tombs that lay closest to the cottage.

He hoped the mists and elms had not quite swallowed him up from Harris's view. After all, he'd no wish to perform for the night and the dead alone (supposing the sexton never came). Harris ought to get some benefit. Besides which, a most gloomy loneliness was come upon him. A melancholy loneliness, the like of which he'd never known.

'Harris!' he called softly; but was too far off to be heard by the physician's son.

Suddenly, he must have passed into a curious nestling of mists. The echo of his drum seemed to have become more distinct. Strange effect of nature. Harris would be interested.

'Harris . . .'

There seemed to be layers in the mist . . . first soft and tumbled, then smooth.

These smooth patches, he fancied he glimpsed through shifting holes. Or believed he did. For once more he seemed to be reflected in them—then lost

from sight—then back again . . . glowing briefly blue
and green.

'Harris . . .'

Now the reflected image stayed longer. Marched
with him . . . drummed with him . . .

Yet in that mirror made of mist, there was a strange
deception. No ointment had been applied to Bostock's face, yet this shadow drummer's narrow brow
and sunken cheeks were glowing with—

'Harris!'

But Harris never heard him. Harris had fled.
Harris, from his watching place beyond the graves,
had observed that his gleaming friend had attracted
a companion. Another, palely glowing grenadier!

'Harris—Harris—' moaned the painted Bostock as
the terrible drummer paused and stared at him with
eyes that were no eyes but patches of blackness in a
tragic, mouldered face.

Suddenly, the terrified boy recovered the use of
his legs; or, rather, his legs recovered the use of the
boy. And wrenched him violently away.

In truth, he did not know he'd begun to run, till
running he'd been for seconds. Like a wounded
firefly, he twittered and stumbled and wove wildly
among the graves. All his frantic daring was now
abruptly changed into its reverse. Frantic terror
engulfed him—and was doubled each time he looked
back.

And the phantom drummer was following . . .
drumming as it came . . . staring as if with reproach
for the living boy's mockery of its unhappy state.

Now out of the churchyard fled the boy, much
hampered by his ridiculous costume and overlarge

drum, which thumped as his knees struck it—like a huge, hollow heart.

Into the lane whence he'd come, he rushed. He might have been a craven soldier, flying some scene of battle, with his spectral conscience in pursuit.

At the end of the lane, he paused; groaned 'Harris!' miserably once more; but no Harris answered; only the drum . . . drum . . . drum! of the phantom he'd drawn in his wake.

Very striking was its aspect now, as it drifted out of the shadows of the lane. Its clothing was threadbare—and worse. Its cap was on the large size . . . as were the cuffs that hung upon the ends of its bone-thin fingers like strange, frayed mouths.

And on its face was a look of glaring sadness, most sombre to behold.

Not that Bostock was much inclined to behold it, or to make its closer acquaintance in any way.

Yet even though he'd turned and fled, trembling on, the tragic drummer's face remained printed on his inward eye . . .

'I'm going home—going home!' sobbed Bostock as he ran. 'You can't come with me there!'

But the sound of the drum grew no fainter . . . and the spectre followed on.

'What do you want with me? What have I done? I'm Dick Bostock—and nought to you! Dick Bostock, d'you hear? A stranger—no more!'

Drum . . . drum . . . drum! came on behind him; and, when the boy helplessly turned, he saw on the phantom's face a look of unearthly hope!

'This is my home!' sobbed the boy at last, when he

came to the comfortable little road he knew so well.
'Leave me now!'

He stumbled down the row of stout flint cottages
till he came to his own. With shaking fingers, he
unlatched his garden gate.

'Leave me! Leave me!'

Drum . . . drum . . . drum! came relentless down
the street.

'Now I'm safe—now I'm safe!' moaned Bostock,
for he'd come to the back of his house.

There, under the roof, was his bedroom window,
in which a candle warmly burned.

Of a sudden: the terrible drumming stopped.
'Thank God!' whispered Bostock.

He drew in his breath, prayed—and looked behind
him.

'Thank God!' he whispered again: the phantom
was gone.

Now he turned to his home and hastened to climb
up an old apple tree that had ever served him for
stairs. He reached the longed-for window. He looked
within. He gave a groan of terror and dismay.

In his room, seated on his bed, looking out of his
window—was the horrible drummer again.

And, as the living boy stared palely in, so the dead
one stared out . . . then, it lifted up its arm and
pointed.

It pointed unmistakably past the unhappy Bostock
. . . over his shoulder and towards the churchyard
whence it had come.

There was no doubt of its meaning. None at all.
Bostock must fill the place left vacant in the churchyard. His own had just been taken.

Never was a live boy worse situated. Never had an apple tree borne whiter fruit . . . that now dropped down, dismally phosphorescent, to the cold, damp ground.

The miserable Bostock, phosphorescent as ever, stood forlornly under the apple tree. The phantom had caught him and trapped him most malevolently.

To appear as he was, at his own front door, was more than his courage or compassion allowed.

His father and mother's fury on his awesome appearance, he could have endured. But there was worse than that. Would they not have died of fright when they faced his usurper—the grim inhabitant of his room—that other shining drummer boy?

Tears of misery and despair stood in his eyes, ran over and fell upon his tingling hands.

Harris! He must go to Harris, the physician's large-headed son. Wise old Harris . . .

He crept out into the road and ran deviously to a prosperous house that stood on the corner. Candles were shining in the parlour window and the good doctor and his lady were sat on either side of their fire. But Harris was not with them. Bostock flitted to the back of the house. Harris's bedroom was aglow. He had returned.

'Harris!' called Bostock, urgently. But Harris's window was tight shut, against the damp air . . . and more.

'Harris! For pity's sake, Harris!'

No answer. Harris had heard nothing save, most likely, the uneasy pounding of his own heart.

Desperately, Bostock cast about for pebbles to fling at the window. With no success. What then?

The drum! He would tap on the drum. Harris would hear that. For certain sure, Harris would hear that.

And Harris did hear it. Came to his window aghast. Ever of a studious, pimplish disposition; his spots burned now like little fiery mountains in the ashes of his face. Not knowing which drummer he was beholding, he took it for the worse. Bostock would have shouted; Bostock would have thrown pebbles at the window . . . not beaten the evil drum!

He vanished from his window with a soundless cry of dismay. His curtain was drawn rapidly and Bostock—faintly shining Bostock—was left, rejected of the living.

So he began to walk, choosing the loneliest, darkest ways. Twice he frightened murmuring lovers, winding softly home. But he got no pleasure from it . . .

Glumly, he wondered if this was a sign of slipping into true ghostliness.

This mournful thought led to another, even sadder. He wondered if the phantom in his bedroom was now losing its weird glow, and generally filling out into a perfect likeness of the boy whose place it had stolen.

Very likely. Nature and un-nature, so to speak, were disagreeably tidy. They cared for nothing left over. Vague and confused memories of Dr Barron's classroom, sleep-provoking voice filled his head . . . and he wished he'd attended more carefully. He felt the lack of solid learning in which he might have found an answer to his plight.

Ghosts, phantoms, unquiet spirits of all denominations stalked the earth for a purpose. And until that purpose was achieved, they were doomed to continue in their melancholy office.

This much, Bostock had a grasp of: but if ever Dr Barron had let fall anything further that might have been of help, Bostock could not remember it. Neither tag nor notion nor fleeting word remained in his head. He was alone and shining—and his hands were beginning to burn.

Of a sudden, he found himself in the lane that wound to the north of the church. Back to the churchyard he was being driven, by forces outside his reckoning.

'Goodbye, Harris,' he whispered, as he stumbled through the broken hedge and across the grass towards the night-pierced bulk of the ruined church. 'Goodbye for ever.'

The thick grass muttered against his legs and his drum grumbled softly under his lifting knees.

'Goodbye, light of day; goodbye Dr Barron; goodbye my mother and father; goodbye my friends and enemies; goodbye my cat Jupiter and my dear mice . . . Oh Harris, Harris! Remember me! Remember your young friend Bostock—who went for a ghost and never came back!'

And then, with a pang of bitterness the thought returned that the spectre would have become another Bostock. Harris would have no cause to remember what Harris would never know had gone.

When he found himself among the elms the anger vanished. Instead Bostock sadly, resignedly surveyed his future realm.

There lay the graves, all leaning and tumbled like stone ships, frozen in a stormy black sea. The mists were almost gone and the starlight glimmered coldly down. What was he to do? How best discharge his new office? The drum, that was it, beat the drum and drift uncannily to and fro.

So he began, drum . . . drum . . . drum! But, it must be admitted, he tended to stumble rather than to drift; for, where a phantom might have floated, Bostock trod. Many a time he caught his bruised feet in roots that were more uncanny than he. But there was yet something more frightening than that. His hands were burning more and more.

He tried to subdue the pain by thinking on other things. But what thoughts could come to a boy in a dark churchyard save unwelcome ones?

He gave several dismal groans, even more pitiful than a wandering spirit might have uttered. His poor hands were afire . . .

Water—he must have water! He felt in the long grass for such damp as the mists might have left behind. Too little . . . too little. He ran from grave to grave, laying his hands against the cold, moist stone. To no purpose. He looked to the ragged, broken church . . . Of a sudden, a hope plucked at his heart.

There was to be a christening on the morrow. A fisherman's child . . . Already, it had been delayed for two months on account of a chill. Harris—interested in all such matters—had sagely talked of it. ('In my opinion, they ought to wait another month. But there's no arguing with superstitious fisherfolk! They'll douse the brat on Sunday, come snivel, come sneeze, come galloping decline!')

The font! Maybe it was already filled?

Bostock began to run. A frantic sight, his luminous knees thumped the underside of the drum setting up the rapid thunder of an advance. His luminous sleeves, his gleaming cuffs with his distracted hands held high, flared through the night like shining banners. And, as he passed them by, the old cracked tombstones seemed to gape in amazement—and lean as if to follow.

At last, he reached the church; halted, briefly prayed, and crept inside.

All was gloom and deep shadows, and the night wind blowing through rents in the stone caused the empty pews to creak and sigh as if under the memory of generations of Sunday sleepers . . .

Bostock approached the font. Thank God for Christian fisherfolk! It was filled.

With huge relief, he sank his wretched, shining hands into the icy water. They glimmered against the stone beneath the water like nightmarish fish . . . But oh! the blessed stoppage of the pain!

He stood, staring towards the altar, upon which, from a higher hole in the roof, such light as was in the night sky dropped gently down.

He started; and, in so doing, scraped the drum against the font. It rattled softly through the dark.

What had made him to start? He was not alone in the church. A figure was crouched upon the altar step. A figure seemingly sunk in sleep or prayer or stony brooding . . .

On the sound of the drum, the figure turned— and groaned to its feet.

It was the sour and savage old sexton. Bitter moment for Bostock. Too late now to get any joy out of frightening the old man stupid. Bostock, his hands in the font, was more frightened by far. Unhappily, he awaited the old man's wrath.

But the old man only stood and stared at him. There was no rage in his withered face; only wonderment and fear. Nor was it a sudden fear, such as a man might betray on first seeing a ghost. It was the deep, abiding fear of a man to whom a ghost came often—to plague him on misty Saturday nights. For in the shadow of the church, he took the glimmering Bostock to be that phantom that had troubled him this many a long year. Yet . . . with a difference—

'Into the church?' he whispered. 'Even into the church, now? What does it mean? You never came in the church before. Is it—is it forgiveness, at last?'

Bostock stared at the shrivelled old sexton—that terror of marauding boys. Very miserable and desolate was the ancient wretch. Very pitiful was the hope in his eyes—

'Yes!' cried the sexton, with misguided joy. 'It's forgiveness! I see it in your eyes! Pity! Blessed, blessed pity!'

Fearful to speak, or even to move, Bostock gazed at the old man who now hobbled towards him. There was a look of tarnished radiance on his face as secrets long knotted in his heart began to unravel and give him peace.

'At last my treasure, dear spirit! Now I can go to it! It's all right now? In this holy place, you've come to forgive? My treasure! All these years of waiting for it! All these years of misery . . . all these years of longing . . . How many? Eighteen! But all's forgiven now . . . at last, at last!'

Careless of the raging ointment, Bostock drew his hands out of the font as the old man tottered by, mumbling and gabbling as he went.

For the old man did pass him by, his face quite transfigured by yearning and relief. He went out into the tumbledown churchyard, clucking over the neglected graves like an ancient gardener, revisiting an overgrown garden he'd once tended well . . .

Absorbed beyond measure, the luminous Bostock followed—straining to catch the drift of the old man's broken words.

There was no doubt now, the ghost had been that of the founding boy who'd long ago drummed for the smugglers. Likewise, there was no doubt that the sexton had brought him to his death.

'I never knew you was ailing, my dear. I never knew the paint was a-poisoning you. I swear I'd never have made you go out when the mists was gone if I'd known! Ask the others—if you're situated to do so. They'll tell you I never knew. Thought you was pretending for more of the haul. Thought your cries and moans were play-acting. Never, never thought you'd die, my dear!'

Thus he mumbled and muttered—half over his shoulder—to what he fancied was the ghost he hoped had forgiven him at last.

For it turned out that this ancient sexton had been of the smugglers himself; and had most cunningly escaped hanging with the rest.

'There, my dear. There's your grave. See—I've tended it all these years . . .'

He paused by a patch of ground where the grass had been newly cut.

'But my treasure . . . now I can go fetch my treasure. Now I can live once more . . . now I can leave this accursed place! A—a house in London, maybe . . . a coach and pair . . . Just for my last years . . . my treasure will make up for all!'

Hastening now, he fumbled among the altar-tombs, heaving at the slabs till at last he came upon the one he sought.

'It's here! It's here!'

With a loud grinding, the slab of stone slid sideways and fell upon the ground. The old man reached within and fumbled for the hoard that had waited in the earth for eighteen years.

Bostock moved nearer. He strained to see. He sniffed the heavy air. His heart contracted in grief for the luckless sexton.

From the smugglers' hiding place, came forth only the dismal smell of rotting tea and mouldered tobacco leaf. All had crumbled away.

The old man had begun to sob. A ruinous sound.

Quite consumed with pity, Bostock laid a hand on the sexton's wasted shoulder and muttered:

'I'm sorry . . . truly sorry, sir . . .'

Whereupon the old man whirled round upon him in a sudden access of amazement and fist-shaking rage.

The hand on his shoulder, the voice in his ear had been no ghost's, but those of a mortal boy.

He beheld the fantastic Bostock. An undersized, somewhat timid grenadier whose protruding ears alone prevented his mansize cap from quite extinguishing him.

Was it to this small, mocking villain he'd opened his heart and betrayed it?

He stared—but saw no laughter in Bostock's face. Rather did he see a startled compassion that came in a gentle flood from Bostock's heart and filled up Bostock's eyes—making them to shine softly—and from thence, ran resistless down Bostock's cheeks. The boy was crying for him. The boy had partly understood, and was grieving for the wastage of his poor life, for his heart that had turned to dust—by reason of the haunting of his soul.

'What—what are you doing here, boy?'

Bostock shook his head; made to wipe his eyes, then stared, frightened, at his luminous hand and hid it behind his back.

The sexton went grey with horror—on the memory of an old, old occasion. He gave some four or five harsh, constricted cries—for all the world as if the organ that produced them was stirring after long disuse. Then he partly screamed and partly shouted:

'What have you done with your hands? What—have—you—done? Oh God, you'll die! You'll die again! He died of it! A doctor! Quick—quick! This time, I'll save you! Please God, let me save you this time!'

He reached out and seized the terrified Bostock by a cuff. Now he began to drag him, as fast as his hobble would permit, out of the churchyard and towards Brighthelmstone. And all the while, he panted; 'Let me save him—let me save him!'

Tremendous sight . . . remarked on for years afterwards by startled tavern-leavers who'd glimpsed the bounding, limping old man and the phosphorescent boy.

A sight never to be forgotten—least of all by Dr

Harris at whose door the sexton banged and kicked till it was opened.

Before he could be gainsaid, he'd dragged the wretched Bostock in and begged the doctor to try to save him.

'What's amiss? What's amiss, then?'

'He'll die—he'll die!' wept the sexton. 'Just like the other one!'

Then out tumbled the sexton's grim secret while the doctor's household listened in judgement and in pity. For though the old man had been a murderer— had done for the foundling by his eager greed—it was plain to all he'd paid a high price for his crime.

'This boy will be saved,' muttered Dr Harris, as he began treating those hands inflamed by the evil ointment. 'But may God forgive you for that other one.'

Now it seemed to Bostock as he sat, with wise old nightgowned Harris come down to be by his side, that the night was grown suddenly warmer. The fire burned bright—as if an obstruction had been lifted off the chimney . . .

He was not alone in noticing this. It was remarked on by the doctor, who diagnosed a sudden, beneficial draught. Likewise, it was observed by the sexton—the confessed murderer—who peered at it, then glanced towards the window as if the cause was passing down the street. For he nodded . . .

And though Bostock, who followed his gaze, saw nothing but darkness, he knew that the usurping phantom had at last slipped away, its purpose achieved, its office at full term.

So did the phantom drummer boy haunt the

churchyard no more? Did it never stalk on misty Saturday nights? And was its drum heard never again to echo across the tumbled tombs? Yes: but only once more—and that not so long after.

D'you remember when they buried the old sexton at Hove? The old sexton who from that night on had seemed to give up interest in life let alone bedevilling the young boys who came inside his domain. It was late on a Saturday night, and the sea mists were coming up.

D'you remember the sound of drumming that accompanied his coffin? And the gentle beating as it was lowered into its grave? It had a strangely forgiving sound ... They say it was a retreat that was being beaten; but to Bostock and Harris it sounded more like a welcome.

*   *   *

LEON GARFIELD once said, 'There is nothing nicer than to be frightened by a book.' He certainly did his best to achieve this for his readers in the stories he wrote during a busy career that made him one of Britain's leading writers of children's fiction. As a young man he was an art student, and when he joined the Army he was drafted into the Medical Corps on the theory, he said, that art students know about human anatomy! He was put into a laboratory and taught biochemistry, which he later used to make a living as a teacher while he wrote stories and tried to get them published. He eventually succeeded with books such as *Devil-in-the-Fog, Mister Corbett's Ghost* and *The Ghost Downstairs* which brought him several awards, including the Library Association Carnegie Medal in 1971 and the Children's Literature Association Award in 1987. Leon Garfield believed that a ghost only appears to the person for whom it is relevant—though the world is full of the spirits of dead people, we may not notice one *until* we bump into the phantom of someone we used to know. Scary thought, isn't it?

THE THIRTEENTH DAY OF CHRISTMAS

Isaac Asimov

Larry the son of a New York detective, is a smart kid who fancies himself as a young Sherlock Holmes. When the family Christmas Day is well and truly messed up because of a terrorist bomb threat at the United Nations building, which means the call of duty for Dad—and yet nothing happens— Larry reckons the danger is still far from over. Someone needs to solve the mystery: and he decided it had better be him before what is already a scary festive season becomes really deadly *instead.*

*   *   *

This was one year when we were glad Christmas Day was over.

It had been a grim Christmas Eve, and I was just as glad I don't stay awake listening for sleigh bells any more. After all, I'm about ready to get out of junior high. But then, I kind of stayed awake listening for bombs.

We stayed up till midnight of Christmas *Day*, though, up till the last minute of it, Mom and I. Then Dad called and said, 'Okay, it's over. Nothing's happened. I'll be home as soon as I can.'

Mom and I danced around for a while as though Santa Claus had just come, and then, after about an hour, Dad came home and I went to bed and slept fine.

You see, it's special in our house. Dad's a detective on the force and these days, with terrorists and bombings, it can get pretty hairy. So when, on December 20th, warnings reached headquarters that there would be a Christmas Day bombing at the Soviet offices in the United Nations, it had to be taken seriously.

The entire force was put on the alert and the FBI came in too. The Soviets had their own security, I guess, but none of it satisfied Dad.

The day before Christmas he said, 'If someone is crazy enough to want to plant a bomb and if he's not too worried about getting caught afterwards, he's likely to be able to do it no matter what precautions we take.'

Mom said, 'I suppose there's no way of knowing who it is.'

Dad shook his head. 'Letters from newspapers pasted on paper. No fingerprints; only smudges. Common stuff we can't trace and he said it would be the only warning, so we won't get anything else to work on. What can we do?'

Mom said, 'Well, it must be someone who doesn't like the Russians, I guess.'

Dad said, 'That doesn't narrow it much. Of course, the Soviets say it's a Zionist threat, and we've got to keep an eye on the Jewish Defence League.'

I said, 'Gee, Dad, that doesn't make much sense. The Jewish people wouldn't pick Christmas Day to do it, would they? It doesn't mean anything to them, and it doesn't mean anything to the Soviet Union, either. They're officially atheist.'

Dad said, 'You can't reason that out to the Russians. Now why don't you turn in, because tomorrow may be a bad day all round, Christmas or not.'

Then he left, and he was out all Christmas Day, and it was pretty rotten. We didn't even open any presents, just sat listening to the radio which was tuned to an all-day news station.

Then at midnight, when Dad called and said nothing had happened, we breathed again, but I still forgot to open my presents.

That didn't come till the morning of the 26th. We made *that* day Christmas. Dad had a day off and Mom baked the turkey a day late. It wasn't till after dinner that we talked about it again.

Mom said, 'I suppose the person, whoever it was, couldn't find any way of planting the bomb once the Department drew the security strings tight.'

Dad smiled, as though he appreciated Mom's loyalty. He said, 'I don't think you can make security that tight, but what's the difference? There was no bomb. Maybe it was a bluff. After all, it did disrupt the city a bit and it gave the Soviet people at the United Nations some sleepless nights, I bet. That might have been almost as good for the bomber as letting the bomb go off.'

I said, 'If he couldn't do it on Christmas Day, maybe he'll do it another time. Maybe he just said Christmas to get everyone keyed up and then, after they relax, he'll—'

Dad gave me one of his little pushes on the side of my head. 'You're a cheerful one, Larry. No, I don't think so. Real bombers value the sense of power. When they say something is going to happen at a certain time, it's got to be that time or it's no fun for them.'

I was still suspicious, but the days passed and there was no bombing and the Department gradually got back to normal. The FBI left and even the Soviet people seemed to forget about it, according to Dad.

On January 2 the Christmas-New Year's vacation was over and I went back to school, and we started rehearsing our Christmas pageant. We didn't call it that, of course, because we're not supposed to have religious celebrations at school, what with the separation of church and state. We just made an elaborate show out of the song, 'The Twelve Days of Christmas', which doesn't have any religion to it—just presents.

There were twelve of us kids, each one singing a particular line every time it came up and then coming in all together on the 'partridge in a pear tree'. I was number five, singing 'Five gold rings' because I was still a boy soprano and I could hit that high note pretty nicely, if I do say so myself.

Some kids didn't know why Christmas had twelve days, but I explained that on the twelfth day after Christmas, which was January 6, the Three Wise Men arrived with gifts for the Christ child. Naturally, it was on January 6 that we put on the show in the auditorium, with as many parents there as wanted to come.

Dad got a few hours off and was sitting in the audience with Mom. I could see him getting set to hear his son's clear high note for the last time because next year my voice changes or I know the reason why.

Did you ever get an idea in the middle of a stage show and have to continue, no matter what?

We were only on the second day with its 'two turtle-doves' when I thought, 'Oh, my, it's the *thirteenth* day of Christmas.' The whole world was shaking around me and I couldn't do a thing but stay on the stage and sing about five gold rings.

I didn't think they'd ever get to those 'twelve drummers drumming'. It was like having itching powder on instead of underwear—I couldn't stand still. Then, when the last note was out, while they were still applauding, I broke away, went jumping down the steps from the platform and up the aisle, calling, 'Dad!'

He looked startled, but I grabbed him, and I think I was babbling so fast that he could hardly understand.

I said, 'Dad, Christmas isn't the same day everywhere. It could be one of the Soviet's own people. They're officially atheist, but maybe one of them is religious and he wants to place the bomb for that reason. Only he would be a member of the *Russian* Orthodox Church. They don't go by our calendar.'

'What?' said Dad, looking as though he didn't understand a word I was saying.

'It's *so*, Dad. I read about it. The Russian Orthodox Church is still on the Julian Calendar, which the west gave up for the Gregorian Calendar centuries ago. The Julian Calendar is thirteen days behind ours. The Russian Orthodox Christmas is on *their* December 25, which is *our* January 7. It's *tomorrow*.'

He didn't believe me, just like that. He looked it up in the almanac, then he called up someone in the Department who was Russian Orthodox.

He was able to get the Department moving again. They talked to the Soviets, and once the Soviets stopped talking about Zionists and looked at themselves, they got the man. I don't know what they did with him, but there was no bombing on the thirteenth day of Christmas, either.

The Department wanted to give me a new bicycle for Christmas, but I turned it down. I told them I was just doing my duty.

*　　*　　*

ISAAC ASIMOV became fascinated with stories of mystery and science fiction in the magazines which his father sold in his shop in New York. Like Larry in the story, he was a bright kid at school and university and later became a professor of biochemistry at Boston University School of Medicine—following in the footsteps of Leon Garfield across the Atlantic. Asimov began writing while he was a lecturer, and it was his science fiction stories in particular which helped to make him the most influential US sf writer of his time. He became popular for his series of Robot stories in which he set out the 'Three Laws of Robotics' and the equally-celebrated Foundation series about a Galactic Empire of the future. Isaac Asimov also wrote a series of sf stories for younger readers featuring David Starr, a Space Ranger, and a number of crime and mystery tales for both age groups which appeared in the *Ellery Queen Mystery Magazine*. 'The Thirteenth Day of Christmas' is typical of these, and young Larry is in the same tradition as a number of other young sleuths, including Mark Twain's Tom Sawyer, Eden Phillpotts' Vincent Peters and even Ellery Queen Jr., who appeared in the same magazine.

HUSH!

Zenna Henderson

June is babysitting Dubby Warren, a sickly little boy with a plaintive voice but the wisest eyes you ever saw in a child. When Dubby runs out of games to play and June still hasn't finished her homework, she tells him to use his imagination to amuse himself a while longer. But when the strange kid comes up with a machine that looks like a vacuum cleaner on slides with a mind all of its own which he calls the 'Noise Eater', June suddenly finds herself in the most scary nightmare for real that any babysitter could possibly imagine . . .

*   *   *

June sighed and brushed her hair back from her eyes automatically as she marked her place in her geometry book with one finger and looked through the dining-room door at Dubby lying on the front-room couch.

'Dubby, *please*,' she pleaded. 'You promised your mother that you'd be quiet tonight. How can you get over your cold if you bounce around making so much noise?'

Dubby's fever-bright eyes peered from behind his tented knees where he was holding a tin truck which he hammered with a toy guitar.

'I am quiet, June. It's the truck that made the noise. See?' And he banged on it again. The guitar splintered explosively and Dubby blinked in surprise. He was wavering between tears at the destruction and pleased laughter for the awful noise it made. Before he could decide, he began to cough, a deep-chested pounding cough that shook his small body unmercifully.

'That's just about enough out of you, Dubby,' said June firmly, clearing the couch of toys and twitching the covers straight with a practised hand. 'You have to go to your room in just fifteen minutes anyway— or right now if you don't settle down. Your mother will be calling at seven to see if you're okay. I don't want to have to tell her you're worse because you wouldn't be good. Now read your book and keep quiet. I've got work to do.'

There was a brief silence broken by Dubby's sniffling and June's scurrying pencil. Then Dubby began to chant:

> 'Shrimp boatses running a dancer tonight
> Shrimp boatses running a dancer tonight
> *Shrimp* boatses *run*ning a *dancer tonight*
> SHRIMP BOATses RUNning a DANcer
>   toNIGHT—'

'Dub-by!' called June, frowning over her paper at him.

'That's not noise,' protested Dubby. 'It's singing. *Shrimp boatses*—' The cough caught him in midphrase and June busied herself providing Kleenexes and comfort until the spasm spent itself.

'See?' she said. 'Your cough thinks it's noise.'

'Well, what can I do then?' fretted Dubby, bored by four days in bed and worn out by the racking cough that still shook him. 'I can't sing and I can't play. I want something to do.'

'Well,' June searched the fertile pigeonholes of her babysitter's repertoire and came up with an idea that Dubby had once originated himself and dearly loved. 'Why not play-like? Play-like a zoo. I think a green giraffe with a mop for a tail and roller skates for feet would be nice, don't you?'

Dubby considered the suggestion solemnly. 'If he had egg beaters for ears,' he said, overly conscious as always of ears, because of the trouble he so often had with his own.

'Of course he does,' said June. 'Now you play-like one.'

'Mine's a lion,' said Dubby, after mock consideration. 'Only he has a flag for a tail—a pirate flag—and he wears yellow pyjamas and aeroplane wings sticking out of his back and his ears turn like propellers.'

'That's a good one,' applauded June. 'Now mine is an eagle with rainbow wings and roses growing around his neck. And the only thing he ever eats is the song of birds, but the birds are scared of him and so he's hungry nearly all the time—pore ol'iggle!'

Dubby giggled. 'Play-like some more,' he said, settling back against the pillows.

'No, it's your turn. Why don't you play-like by yourself now? I've just got to get my geometry done.'

Dubby's face shadowed and then he grinned. 'Okay.'

June went back to the table, thankful that Dubby was a nice kid and not like some of the brats she had met in her time. She twined both legs around the legs of her chair, running both hands up through her hair. She paused before tackling the next problem to glance in at Dubby. A worry nudged at her heart as she saw how pale and fine-drawn his features were. It seemed, every time she came over, he was more nearly transparent.

She shivered a little as she remembered her mother saying, 'Poor child. He'll never have to worry about old age. Have you noticed his eyes, June? He has wisdom in them now that no child should have. He has looked too often into the Valley.'

June sighed and turned to her work.

The heating system hummed softly and the out-of-joint day settled into a comfortable accustomed evening.

Mrs Warren rarely ever left Dubby because he was ill so much of the time, and she practically never left him until he was settled for the night. But today when June got home from school, her mother had told her to call Mrs Warren.

'Oh, June,' Mrs Warren had appealed over the phone, 'could you possibly come over right now?'

'Now?' asked June, dismayed, thinking of her hair and nails she'd planned to do, and the tentative date with Larryanne to hear her new album.

'I hate to ask it,' said Mrs Warren. 'I have no patience with people who make last minute arrangements, but Mr Warren's mother is very ill again and we just have to go over to her house. We wouldn't trust Dubby with anyone but you. He's got that nasty bronchitis again, so we can't take him with us. I'll get home as soon as I can, even if Orin has to stay. He's home from work right now, waiting for me. So please come, June!'

'Well,' June melted to the tears in Mrs Warren's voice. She could let her hair and nails and album go and she could get her geometry done at the Warrens' place. 'Well, okay. I'll be right over.'

'Oh, bless you, child,' cried Mrs Warren. Her voice faded away from the phone. 'Orin, she's coming—' and the receiver clicked.

'June!' He must have called several times before June began to swim back up through the gloomy haze of the new theorem.

'Joo-un!' Dubby's plaintive voice reached down to her and she sighed in exasperation. She had nearly figured out how to work the problem.

'Yes, Dubby.' The exaggerated patience in her voice signalled her displeasure to him.

'Well,' he faltered, 'I don't want to play-like any more. I've used up all my thinkings. Can I make something now? Something for true?'

'Without getting off the couch?' asked June cautiously, wise from past experience.

'Yes,' grinned Dubby.

'Without my to-ing-and fro-ing to bring you stuff?' she questioned, still wary.

'Uh-huh,' giggled Dubby.

'What can you make for true without anything to make it with?' June asked sceptically.

Dubby laughed. 'I just thought it up.' Then all in

one breath, unable to restrain his delight: 'It's-really-kinda-like-play-like,   but-I'm   going-to-make-something-that-isn't-like-anything-real-so   it'll-be-for-true, cause-it-won't-be-play-like-anything-that's-real!'

'Huh? Say that again,' June challenged. 'I bet you can't do it.'

Dubby was squirming with excitement. He coughed tentatively, found it wasn't a prelude to a full production and said: 'I can't say it again, but I can do it, I betcha. Last time I was sick, I made up some new magic words. They're real good. I betcha they'll work real good like anything.'

'Okay, go ahead and make something,' said June. 'Just so it's quiet.'

'Oh, it's *real* quiet,' said Dubby in a hushed voice. 'Exter quiet. I'm going to make a Noise-eater.'

'A Noise-eater?'

'Uh-huh!' Dubby's eyes were shining. 'It'll eat up all the noises. I can make lotsa racket then, 'cause it'll eat it all up and make it real quiet for you so's you can do your jommety.'

'Now that's right thunkful of you, podner,' drawled June. 'Make it a good one, because little boys make a lot of noise.'

'Okay.' And Dubby finally calmed down and settled back against his pillows.

The heating system hummed. The old refrigerator in the kitchen cleared its throat and added its chirking throb to the voice of the house. The mantel clock tocked firmly to itself in the front room. June was absorbed in her homework when a flutter of movement at her elbow jerked her head up.

'Dubby!' she began indignantly.

'Shh!' Dubby pantomimed, finger to lips, his eyes wide with excitement. He leaned against June, his fever radiating like a small stove through his pyjamas and robe. His breath was heavy with the odour of illness as he put his mouth close to her ear and barely whispered.

'I made it. The Noise-eater. He's asleep now. Don't make a noise or he'll get you.'

'I'll get you, too,' said June. 'Play-like is play-like, but you get right back on that couch!'

'I'm too scared,' breathed Dubby. 'What if I cough?'

'You will cough if you—' June started in a normal tone, but Dubby threw himself into her lap and muffled her mouth with his small hot hand. He was trembling.

'Don't! Don't!' he begged frantically. 'I'm scared. How do you un-play-like? I didn't know it'd work so good!'

There was a *choonk* and a slither in the front room. June strained her ears, alarm stirring in her chest.

'Don't be silly,' she whispered. 'Play-like isn't for true. There's nothing in there to hurt you.'

A sudden succession of musical pings startled June and threw Dubby back into her arms until she recognised Mrs Warren's bedroom clock striking seven o'clock—early as usual. There was a soft, drawn-out slither in the front room and then silence.

'Go on, Dubby. Get back on the couch like a nice child. We've played long enough.'

'You take me.'

June herded him ahead of her, her knees bumping his reluctant back at every step until he got a good look at the whole front room. Then he sighed and relaxed.

'He's gone,' he said normally.

'Sure he is,' replied June. 'Play-like stuff always goes away.' She tucked him under his covers. Then, as if hoping to brush his fears—and hers—away, by calmly discussing it, 'What did he look like?'

'Well, he had a body like Mother's vacuum cleaner—the one that lies down on the floor—and his legs were like my sledge, so he could slide on the floor, and had a nose like the hose on the cleaner only he was able to make it long or short when he wanted to.'

Dubby, overstrained, leaned back against his pillows.

The mantel clock began to boom the hour deliberately.

'And he had little eyes like the light inside the refrigerator—'

June heard a *choonk* at the hall door and glanced up. Then with fear-stiffened lips, she continued for him, 'And ears like TV antennae because he needs good ears to find the noises.' And watched, stunned, as the round metallic body glided across the floor on shiny runners and paused in front of the clock that was deliberating on the sixth stroke.

The long, wrinkly trunk-like nose on the front of the thing flashed upward. The end of it shimmered, then melted into the case of the clock. And the seventh stroke never began. There was a soft sucking sound and the nose dropped free. On the mantel, the hands of the clock dropped soundlessly to the bottom of the dial.

In the tight circle of June's arms, Dubby whimpered. June clapped her hand over his mouth. But his shoulders began to shake and he rolled frantic imploring eyes at her as another coughing spell began. He couldn't control it.

June tried to muffle the sound with her shoulder, but over the deep, hawking convulsions, she heard the *choonk* and slither of the creature and screamed as she felt it nudge her knee. Then the long snout nuzzled against her shoulder and she heard a soft hiss as it touched the straining throat of the coughing child. She grabbed the horribly vibrating thing and tried to pull it away, but Dubby's cough cut off in mid-spasm.

In the sudden quiet that followed she heard a gurgle like a straw in the bottom of a soda glass and Dubby folded into himself like an empty laundry bag. June tried to straighten him against the pillows, but he slid laxly down.

June stood up slowly. Her dazed eyes wandered trance-like to the clock, then to the couch, then to the horrible thing that lay beside it. Its glowing eyes were blinking and its ears shifting planes—probably to locate sound.

Her mouth opened to let out the terror that was constricting her lungs, and her frantic scream coincided with the shrill clamour of the telephone. The Eater hesitated, then slid swiftly towards the repeated ring. In the pause after the party line's four identifying rings, it stopped and June clapped both hands over her mouth, her eyes dilated with paralysed terror.

The ring began again. June caught Dubby up into her arms and backed slowly towards the front door. The Eater's snout darted out to the telephone and the ring stilled without even an after-resonance.

The latch of the front door gave a rasping click under June's trembling hand. Behind her, she heard the *choonk* and horrible slither as the Eater lost interest in the silenced telephone. She whirled away from the door, staggering off balance under the limp load of Dubby's body. She slipped to one knee, spilling the child to the floor with a thump. The Eater slid towards her, pausing at the hall door, its ears tilting and moving.

June crouched on her knees, staring, one hand caught under Dubby. She swallowed convulsively, then cautiously withdrew her hand. She touched Dubby's bony little chest. There was no movement. She hesitated indecisively, then backed away, eyes intent on the Eater.

Her heart drummed in her burning throat. Her blood roared in her ears. The starchy *krunkle* of her wide skirt rattled in the stillness. The fibres of the rug murmured under her knees and toes. She circled wider, wider, the noise only loud enough to hold the Eater's attention—not to attract him to her. She backed guardedly into the corner by the radio. Calculatingly, she reached over and clicked it on, turning the volume dial as far as it would go.

The Eater slid tentatively towards her at the click of the switch. June backed slowly away, eyes intent on the creature. The sudden insane blare of the radio hit her an almost physical blow. The Eater glided up close against the vibrating cabinet, its snout lifting and drinking in the horrible cacophony of sound.

June lurched for the front door, wrenching frantically at the door knob. She stumbled outside, slamming the door behind her. Trembling, she sank to the top step, wiping the cold sweat from her face with the under side of her skirt. She shivered in the sharp cold, listening to the raucous outpouring from the radio that boomed so loud it was no longer intelligible.

She dragged herself to her feet, pausing irresolutely, looking around at the huddled houses, each set on its own acre of weeds and lawn. They were all dark in the early winter evening.

June gave a little moan and sank on the step again, hugging herself desperately against the penetrating chill. It seemed an eternity that she crouched there before the radio cut off in mid-note.

Fearfully, she roused and pressed her face to one of the door panes. Dimly through the glass curtains she could see the Eater, sluggish and swollen, lying quietly by the radio. Hysteria was rising for a moment, but she resolutely knuckled the tears from her eyes.

The headlights scythed around the corner, glittering swiftly across the blank windows next door as the car crunched into the Warrens' driveway and came to a gravel-skittering stop.

June pressed her hands to her mouth, sure that even through the closed door she could hear the *choonk* and slither of the thing inside as it slid to and fro, seeking sound.

The car door slammed and hurried footsteps

echoed along the path. June made wild shushing motions with her hands as Mrs Warren scurried round the corner of the house.

'June!' Mrs Warren's voice was ragged with worry. 'Is Dubby all right? What are you doing out here? What's wrong with the phone?' She fumbled for the door knob.

'No, no!' June shouldered her roughly aside. 'Don't go in! It'll get you, too!'

She heard a thud just inside the door. Dimly through the glass she saw the flicker of movement as the snout of the Eater raised and wavered towards them.

'June!' Mrs Warren jerked her away from the door. 'Let me in! What's the matter? Have you gone crazy?'

Mrs Warren stopped suddenly, her face whitening. *'What have you done to Dubby, June?'*

The girl gulped with the shock of the accusation. 'I haven't done anything, Mrs Warren. He made a Noise-eater and it—it—' June winced away from the sudden blaze of Mrs Warren's eyes.

'Get away from that door!' Mrs Warren's face was that of a stranger, her words icy and clipped. 'I trusted you with my child. If anything has happened to him—'

'Don't go in—oh, don't go in!' June grabbed at her coat hysterically. 'Please, please wait! Let's get—'

'Let go!' Mrs Warrens' voice grated between her tightly clenched teeth. 'Let me go, you—you—' Her hand flashed out and the crack of her palm against June's cheek was echoed by a *choonk* inside the house. June was staggered by the blow, but she clung to the coat until Mrs Warren pushed her sprawling down the front steps and fumbled at the knob, crying 'Dubby! Dubby!'

June, scrambling up the steps on hands and knees, caught a glimpse of a hovering something that lifted and swayed like a waiting cobra. It was slapped aside by the violent opening of the door as Mrs Warren stumbled into the house, her cries suddenly stilling on her slack lips as she saw her crumpled son by the couch.

She gasped and whispered, 'Dubby!' She lifted him into her arms. His head rolled loosely against her shoulder. Her protesting, 'No, no, no!' merged into half-articulate screams as she hugged him to her.

And from behind the front door there was a *choonk* and a slither.

June lunged forward and grabbed the reaching thing that was homing in on Mrs Warren's hysterical grief. Her hands closed around it convulsively, her whole weight dragging backwards, but it had a strength she couldn't match. Desperately then, her fists clenched, her eyes tight shut, she screamed and screamed and screamed.

The snout looped almost lazily around her straining throat, but she fought her way almost to the front door before the thing held her, feet on the floor, body at an impossible angle and stilled her frantic screams, quieted her straining lungs and sipped the last of her heartbeats, and let her drop.

Mrs Warren stared incredulously at June's crumpled body and the horrible creature that blinked its lights and shifted its antennae questingly. With a muffled gasp, she sagged, knees and waist and neck, and fell soundlessly to the floor.

The refrigerator in the kitchen cleared its throat and the Eater turned from June with a *choonk* and slid away, crossing to the kitchen.

The Eater retracted its snout and slid back from the refrigerator. It lay quietly, its ears shifting from quarter to quarter.

The thermostat in the dining-room clicked and the hot air furnace began to hum. The Eater slid to the wall under the register that was set just below the ceiling. Its snout extended and lifted and narrowed until the end of it slipped through one of the register openings. The furnace hum choked off abruptly and the snout end flipped back into sight.

Then there was quiet, deep and unbroken until the Eater tilted its ears and slid up to Mrs Warren.

In such silence, even a pulse was noise.

There was a sound like a straw in the bottom of a soda glass.

A stillness was broken by the shrilling of a siren on the main highway four blocks away.

A *choonk* and a slither and the metallic bump of runners down the three front steps.

And a quiet, quiet house on a quiet side street. Hush.

*   *   *

ZENNA HENDERSON was a schoolteacher in Arizona before she became a writer and used a lot of her experiences with children in the books and short stories which made her one of America's favourite writers of fantasy. Her first published story, 'Come On, Wagon', was all about a small boy with the power to make his toys move by themselves, while her book *The Anything Box* contained several tales about children with remarkable powers to enter imaginary worlds ('And a Little Child—') and imprison things of evil ('Stevie and the Dark'). Zenna Henderson became even more popular with her series of books about a group of aliens with psychic powers who become stranded on earth and have to survive as best they can among human beings. The complete collection has been brought together as *The People Omnibus.*

SPOTTY POWDER

Roald Dahl

Miranda Piker is a nasty little girl with a smug expression on her face, always boasting about her achievements and never skiving off from school. There's no doubt she's clever, but what makes things worse is that her father is a head-master and just dotes on his obnoxious child. It certainly seems like a challenge for the great Willy Wonka to knock some of the spots off them in his extraordinary factory. Those of you who recognise some of the characters in this story will be interested to know that it was actually written for Charlie and the Chocolate Factory, *but was left out because the author decided that as the book was already full of kids behaving badly, like Mike Teevee, Veruca Salt and Augustus Gloop, Miranda was just one too many for Willy Wonka to cope with. See what you think after Willy has given both father and daughter a little scare—and a taste of their own medicine . . .*

* * *

'This stuff,' said Mr Wonka, 'is going to cause chaos in schools all over the world when I get it in the shops.'

The room they now entered had rows and rows of pipes coming straight up out of the floor. The pipes were bent over at the top and they looked like large walking-sticks. Out of every pipe there trickled a stream of white crystals. Hundreds of Oompa-Loompas were running to and fro, catching the crystals in little golden boxes and stacking the boxes against the walls.

'Spotty Powder!' exclaimed Mr Wonka, beaming at the company. 'There it is! That's it! Fantastic stuff!'

'It looks like sugar,' said Miranda Piker.

'It's *meant* to look like sugar,' Mr Wonka said. 'And it *tastes* like sugar. But it *isn't* sugar. Oh, dear me, no.'

'Then what is it?' asked Miranda Piker, speaking rather rudely.

'That door over there,' said Mr Wonka, turning away from Miranda and pointing to a small red door at the far end of the room, 'leads directly down to the machine that makes the powder. Twice a day, I go down there myself to feed it. But I'm the only one. Nobody ever comes with me.'

They all stared at the little secret door on which it said MOST SECRET—KEEP OUT.

The hum and throb of powerful machinery could be heard coming up from the depths below, and the floor itself was vibrating all the time. The children could feel it through the soles of their shoes.

Miranda Piker now pushed forward and stood in front of Mr Wonka. She was a nasty-looking girl with a smug face and a smirk on her mouth, and whenever she spoke it was always with a voice that seemed to be saying, 'Everybody is a fool except me.'

'OK,' Miranda Piker said, smirking at Mr Wonka. 'So what's the big news? What's this stuff meant to do when you eat it?'

'Ah-ha,' said Mr Wonka, his eyes sparkling with glee. 'You'd never guess that, not in a million years. Now listen. All you have to do is sprinkle it over your cereal at breakfast-time, pretending it's sugar. Then you eat it. And *then*, exactly five seconds after that, you come out in bright red spots all over your face and neck.'

'What sort of silly person wants spots on his face at breakfast-time?' said Miranda Piker.

'Let me finish,' said Mr Wonka. 'So then your mother looks at you across the table and says, "My poor child. You must have chickenpox. You can't possibly go to school today." So you stay at home. But by lunch-time, the spots have all disappeared.'

'Terrific!' shouted Charlie. 'That's just what I want for the day we have exams!'

'That is the ideal time to use it,' said Mr Wonka. 'But you mustn't do it too often or it'll give the game away. Keep it for the really nasty days.'

'Father!' cried Miranda Piker. 'Did you hear what this stuff does? It's shocking! It mustn't be allowed!'

Mr Piker, Miranda's father, stepped forward and faced Mr Wonka. He had a smooth white face like a boiled onion.

'Now see here, Wonka,' he said. 'I happen to be the headmaster of a large school, and I won't allow you to sell this rubbish to the children! It's ... it's criminal! Why, you'll ruin the school-system of the entire country!'

'I hope so,' said Mr Wonka.

'It's *got* to be stopped!' shouted Mr Piker, waving his cane.

'Who's going to stop it?' asked Mr Wonka. 'In *my* factory, I make things to please children. I don't care about grown-ups.'

'I am top of my form,' Miranda Piker said, smirking

at Mr Wonka. 'And I've never missed a day's school
in my life.'

'Then it's time you did,' Mr Wonka said.

'How dare you!' said Mr Piker.

'All holidays and vacations should be stopped!'
cried Miranda. 'Children are meant to work, not
play.'

'Quite right, my girl,' cried Mr Piker, patting
Miranda on the top of the head. 'All work and no
play has made you what you are today.'

'Isn't she wonderful?' said Mrs Piker, beaming at
her daughter.

'Come on then, father!' cried Miranda. 'Let's go
down into the cellar and smash the machine that
makes this dreadful stuff!'

'Forward!' shouted Mr Piker brandishing his cane
and making a dash for the little red door on which
it said MOST SECRET—KEEP OUT.

'Stop!' said Mr Wonka. 'Don't go in there! It's
terribly secret!'

'Let's see you stop us, you old goat!' shouted
Miranda.

'We'll smash it to smithereens!' yelled Mr Piker.
And a few seconds later the two of them had disappeared through the door.

There was a moment's silence.

Then, far off in the distance, from somewhere deep
underground, there came a fearful scream.

'That's my husband!' cried Mrs Piker, going blue
in the face.

There was another scream.

'And that's Miranda!' yelled Mrs Piker, beginning
to hop around in circles.

'What's happening to them? What have you got down there, you dreadful beast?'

'Oh, nothing much,' Mr Wonka answered. 'Just a lot of cogs and wheels and chains and things like that, all going round and round and round.'

'You villain!' she screamed. 'I know your tricks! You're grinding them into powder! In two minutes, my darling Miranda will come pouring out of one of those dreadful pipes, and so will my husband!'

'Of course,' said Mr Wonka. 'That's part of the recipe.'

'It's what!'

'We've got to use one or two schoolmasters occasionally or it wouldn't work.'

'Did you hear him?' shrieked Mrs Piker, turning to the others. 'He admits it! He's nothing but a cold-blooded murderer!'

Mr Wonka smiled and patted Mrs Piker gently on the arm. 'Dear lady,' he said, 'I was only joking.'

'Then why did they scream?' snapped Mrs Piker. 'I distinctly heard them scream!'

'Those weren't screams,' Mr Wonka said. 'They were laughs.'

'My husband never laughs,' said Mrs Piker.

Mr Wonka flicked his fingers, and up came an Oompa-Loompa.

'Kindly escort Mrs Piker to the boiler room,' Mr Wonka said. 'Don't fret, dear lady,' he went on, shaking Mrs Piker warmly by the hand. 'They'll all come out in the wash. There's nothing to worry about. Off you go. Thank you for coming. Farewell! Goodbye! A pleasure to meet you!'

'Listen, Charlie!' said Grandpa Joe. 'The Oompa-Loompas are starting to sing again!'

'Oh, Miranda Mary Piker!' sang the five Oompa-Loompas dancing about and laughing and beating madly on their tiny drums.

'Oh, Miranda Mary Piker,
How could anybody like her,
Such a priggish and revolting little kid.
So we said, "Why don't we fix her
In the Spotty Powder mixer
Then we're bound to like her better
than we did."
Soon this child who is so vicious
Will have gotten quite delicious,
And her classmates will have surely
understood
That instead of saying, "Miranda!
Oh, the beast! We cannot stand her!"
They'll be saying, "Oh, how useful and
how good!"'

*   *   *

ROALD DAHL is probably as popular a children's writer as R.L. Stine—a position he earned because, as he once said, he understood kids and they understood him. On another occasion he said, 'Parents and schoolteachers are the enemy: the adult is the enemy of the child because of the awful process of civilising this thing that is an animal with no manners, no moral sense at all.'

Roald Dahl often behaved as badly as some of the children he wrote about, once mischievously telling an audience of young schoolchildren his own version of *Little Red Riding Hood* which ended with the girl whipping a pistol from her knickers and shooting the wolf—and later being seen in the woods wearing a fur coat! His mother first gave him his love of stories, but he was a nuisance at school—disliked by his teachers because he was always unpredictable—and earned many beatings as a result. Later he got his revenge on such people in his books.

He started his literary career writing adult short stories but, as he put it, when he ran out of plots he turned to children's tales instead. He scored an instant hit with *James and the Giant Peach*, and this and several others, including *Danny, the Champion of the World*, *The BFG* and *Charlie and the Chocolate Factory* (renamed *Willy Wonka and the Chocolate Factory*), have all been made into films. One particular book Roald Dahl discovered when he was young made a lasting impression on him. 'It was by the American writer Ambrose Bierce, a very spooky book called *Can Such Things Be?*' he wrote. 'I didn't like putting the light out at night when I was reading it—I was 17 at the time.' One of the scariest stories from that book follows next—*if* you are brave enough to turn the page . . .

A BABY TRAMP

Ambrose Bierce

Joseph lives in Blackburg, a remote little American town where weird things happen that could have come straight from an X Files story—things like a shower of frogs falling from the sky and a storm of crimson snow. But when a mysterious disease devastates the town and kills off half the population, Jo is left homeless and an orphan. Despite being fostered several times with different people, he cannot resist a strange attraction that draws him back to Blackburg. What awaits Jo there from his past is not only scary but also unexpected.

*   *   *

If you had seen little Jo standing at the street corner in the rain you would hardly have admired him. It was apparently an ordinary autumn rainstorm, but the water which fell upon Jo (who was hardly old enough to be either just or unjust, and so perhaps did not come under the law of impartial distribution) appeared to have some property peculiar to itself: one would have said it was dark and adhesive—sticky. But that could hardly be so, even in Blackburg, where things certainly did occur that were a good deal out of the common.

For example, ten or twelve years before, a shower

of small frogs had fallen, as is credibly attested by a contemporaneous chronicle, the record concluding with a somewhat obscure statement to the effect that the chronicler considered it good growing-weather for Frenchmen.

Some years later Blackburg had a fall of crimson snow; it is cold in Blackburg when winter is on, and the snows are frequent and deep. There can be no doubt of it—the snow in this instance was of the colour of blood and melted into water of the same hue, if water it was, not blood. The phenomenon had attracted wide attention, and science had as many explanations as there were scientists who knew nothing about it. But the men of Blackburg—men who for many years had lived right there where the red snow fell, and might be supposed to know a good deal about the matter—shook their heads and said something would come of it.

And something did, for the next summer was made memorable by the prevalence of a mysterious disease—epidemic, endemic, or the Lord knows what, though the physicians didn't—which carried away a full half of the population. Most of the other half carried themselves away and were slow to return, but finally came back, and were now increasing and multiplying as before, but Blackburg had not since been altogether the same.

Of quite another kind, though equally 'out of the common', was the incident of Hetty Parlow's ghost. Hetty Parlow's maiden name had been Brownon, and in Blackburg that meant more than one would think.

The Brownons had from time immemorial—from the very earliest of the old colonial days—been the leading family of the town. It was the richest and it was the best, and Blackburg would have shed the last drop of its plebeian blood in defence of the Brownon fair fame. As few of the family's members had ever been known to live permanently away from Black-burg, although most of them were educated else-where and nearly all had travelled, there was quite a number of them. The men held most of the public offices, and the women were foremost in all good works. Of these latter, Hetty was most beloved by reason of the sweetness of her disposition, the purity of her character and her singular personal beauty. She married in Boston a young scapegoat named Parlow, and like a good Brownon brought him to Blackburg forthwith and made a man and a town councilman of him. They had a child which they named Joseph and dearly loved, as was then the fashion among parents in all that region. Then they died of the mysterious disorder already mentioned, and at the age of one whole year Joseph set up as an orphan.

Unfortunately for Joseph the disease which had cut off his parents did not stop at that; it went on and extirpated nearly the whole Brownon contingent and its allies by marriage; and those who fled did not return. The tradition was broken, the Brownon estates passed into alien hands and the only Brownons remaining in that place were underground in Oak Hill Cemetery, where, indeed, was a colony of them powerful enough to resist the encroachment of surrounding tribes and hold the best part of the grounds. But about the ghost:

One night, about three years after the death of

Hetty Parlow, a number of the young people of Blackburg were passing Oak Hill Cemetery in a wagon—
if you have been there you will remember that the
road to Greenton runs alongside it on the south.
They had been attending a May Day festival at
Greenton; and that serves to fix the date. Altogether
there may have been a dozen, and a jolly party they
were, considering the legacy of gloom left by the
town's recent sombre experiences. As they passed the
cemetery the man driving suddenly reined in his
team with an exclamation of surprise. It was suf-
ficiently surprising, no doubt, for just ahead, and
almost at the roadside, though inside the cemetery,
stood the ghost of Hetty Parlow. There could be no
doubt of it, for she had been personally known to
every youth and maiden in the party. That established
the thing's identity; its character as ghost was signi-
fied by all the customary signs—the shroud, the long,
undone hair, the 'faraway look'—everything. This
disquieting apparition was stretching out its arms
towards the west, as if in supplication for the evening
star, which, certainly, was an alluring object, though
obviously out of reach. As they all sat silent (so the
story goes) every member of that party of merry-
makers—they had merry-made on coffee and lemon-
ade only—distinctly heard that ghost call the name
'Joey, Joey!' A moment later nothing was there. Of
course one does not have to believe all that.

Now, at that moment, as was afterwards ascer-
tained, Joey was wandering about in the sagebrush
on the opposite side of the continent, near Winnemucca, in the State of Nevada. He had been taken
to that town by some good persons distantly related

to his dead father, and by them adopted and tenderly cared for. But on that evening the poor child had strayed from home and was lost in the desert.

His after history is involved in obscurity and has gaps which conjecture alone can fill. It is known that he was found by a family of Piute Indians, who kept the little wretch with them for a time and then sold him—actually sold him for money to a woman on one of the eastbound trains, at a station a long way from Winnemucca. The woman professed to have made all manner of inquiries, but all in vain: so, being childless and a widow, she adopted him herself. At this point of his career Jo seemed to be getting a long way from the condition of orphanage; the inter-position of a multitude of parents between himself and that woeful state promised him a long immunity from its disadvantages.

Mrs Darnell, his newest mother, lived in Cleveland, Ohio. But her adopted son did not long remain with her. He was seen one afternoon by a policeman, new to that beat, deliberately toddling away from her house, and being questioned answered that he was 'a goin' home.' He must have travelled by rail, some-how, for three days later he was in the town of Whiteville, which, as you know, is a long way from Blackburg. His clothing was in pretty fair condition, but he was sinfully dirty. Unable to give any account of himself he was arrested as a vagrant and sentenced to imprisonment in the Infants' Sheltering Home— where he was washed.

Jo ran away from the Infants' Sheltering Home at Whiteville—just took to the woods one day and the Home knew him no more forever.

We find him next, or rather get back to him, standing forlorn in the cold autumn rain at a suburban street corner in Blackburg; and it seems right to explain now the raindrops falling upon him there were really not dark and gummy; they only failed to make his face and hands less so. Jo was indeed fearfully and wonderfully besmirched, as by the hand of an artist. And the forlorn little tramp had no shoes; his feet were bare, red and swollen, and when he walked he limped with both legs. As to clothing— ah, you would hardly have had the skill to name any single garment that he wore, or say by what magic he kept it upon him. That he was cold all over and all through did not admit of a doubt; he knew it himself. Anyone would have been cold there that evening; but, for that reason, no one else was there. How Jo came to be there himself, he could not for the flickering little life of him have told, even if gifted with a vocabulary exceeding a hundred words. From the way he stared about him one could have seen that he had not the faintest notion of where (nor why) he was.

Yet he was not altogether a fool in his day and generation; being cold and hungry, and still able to walk a little by bending his knees very much indeed and putting his feet down toes first, he decided to enter one of the houses which flanked the street at long intervals and looked so bright and warm. But when he attempted to act upon that very sensible decision a burly dog came bowsing out and disputed his right. Inexpressibly frightened and believing, no doubt (with some reason, too) that brutes without meant brutality within, he hobbled away from all the houses, and with grey, wet fields to right of him and grey, wet fields to left of him—with the rain half blinding him and the night coming in mist and darkness, held his way along the road that leads to Greenton. That is to say, the road leads those to Greenton who succeed in passing the Oak Hill Cemetery. A considerable number every year do not.

Jo did not.

They found him there the next morning, very wet, very cold, but no longer hungry. He had apparently entered the cemetery gate—hoping, perhaps, that it led to a house where there was no dog—and gone blundering about in the darkness, falling over many a grave, no doubt, until he had tired of it all and given up. The little body lay upon one side, with one soiled cheek upon one soiled hand, the other hand tucked away among the rags to make it warm, the other cheek washed clean and white at last, as for a kiss from one of God's great angels. It was observed— though nothing was thought of it at the time, the body being as yet unidentified—that the little fellow was lying upon the grave of Hetty Parlow. The grave, however, had not opened to receive him. That is a circumstance which, without actual irreverence, one may wish had been ordered otherwise.

*   *   *

AMBROSE BIERCE, whose stories so scared Roald Dahl, had a very unhappy childhood in Ohio. He was one of eleven children, all named with the letter 'A' by their oddball father who was apparently a religious fanatic. This made Bierce hate his family and many of his later stories deal with unhappy families who rob, steal and even murder one another. The children in these stories also do terrible things and more often than not escape without punishment.

For a time Ambrose Bierce worked as a journalist in San Francisco; later he became famous for his satirical stories which earned him the nickname of 'Bitter Bierce'. Following the great success of *Can Such Things Be?* in 1893, he published the *Devil's Dictionary* in which he described childhood as, 'the period of human life intermediate between the idiocy of infancy and the folly of youth—two removes from the sin of manhood and three from the remorse of age.' In time, his horror stories made him as highly regarded as his fellow American, Edgar Allan Poe. But he was always a restless man, and in 1913 he set off for Mexico where a civil war was raging, looking for inspiration. Instead, he disappeared without trace and was never heard of again. It has been suggested—in true *X Files* tradition—that he may have been abducted by aliens . . .

THE MAN UPSTAIRS

Ray Bradbury

Douglas is fascinated by the way his grandmother dissects chickens, carefully removing all the fleshy inside bits before putting them on to cook. He can hardly take his eyes off her when she is busy with one of her sharp kitchen knives, slicing away at the birds. When the strange Mr Koberman arrives to rent their upstairs room and then acts in a most mysterious way, it seems to Douglas that he may require one of grandma's sharpest knives to open up the secret life of this very scary person.

*   *   *

He remembered how carefully and expertly Grandmother would fondle the cold cut guts of the chicken and withdraw the marvels therein; the wet shining loops of meat-smelling intestine, the muscled lump of heart, the gizzard with the collection of seeds in it. How neatly and nicely Grandma would slit the chicken's breast and push her fat little hand in to deprive it of its medals. These would be segregated, some in pans of water, others in paper to be thrown to the dog later, perhaps. And then the ritual of taxidermy, stuffing the bird with watered, seasoned bread, and performing surgery with a swift, bright needle, stitch after pulled tight stitch.

But for all the miracle of surgery, the bird would never survive the operation. It was only transported immediately into a hell and poked and basted and cooked until such time as the other surgeons gathered at the festive board and took up their scalpels to attack.

This was one of the prime thrills of Douglas's eleven-year-old life span.

The knife collection, itself, was an intrigue.

It lay abed in the various squeaking drawers of the large wooden kitchen table. A magic table, from which Grandmama, admittedly a rather kindly, gentle-faced and white-haired old witch, would draw paraphernalia for her miracles. The knives seemed to be most important in the dissection and investigation of chicken and other like fowl.

Altogether, moving his small lips, Douglas counted twenty knives of varying shapes and sizes. And each was unfailingly polished into a sharp mirror in which he could find his red hair and freckles distorted brilliantly.

He was to be quiet while Grandmama worked over her split animals. You could stand across the table from her, your nose tucked over the edge, watching, but any loose boy talk might interfere with the spell. It was a wonder watching Grandma brandish silver shakers over the bird, supposedly sprinkling showers of mummy-dust and pulverised Indian bones, muttering mystical verses under her toothless breath.

Douglas at last gathered courage under him like a coiled spring and let fly with:

'Grammy, am I like that inside?' He pointed at the chicken.

'Like what, child?'

'Am I like *that*, inside?'

'Yes; a little more orderly and presentable, but just about the same—'

'And more *of* it,' added Douglas, proud of his guts.

'Yes,' said Grandma. 'More of it.'

'Grandpa has lots more than me. His sticks out in front so he can rest his elbows on it, Grammy.'

Grandma laughed and shook her head.

Douglas said, 'And Lucie Williams, down the street, she—'

'Hush, child!' cried Grandma.

'But she's got—'

'Never you mind what she's got! That's different. You just shush up about Lucie!'

'But why is *she* different?'

'A darning-needle dragon-fly is coming by some day soon and sew up your mouth,' said Grandma, firmly.

Douglas retreated immediately, then thoughtfully came back with, 'How do you *know* I've got insides like that, Grandma?'

'I just know, that's all. Go 'way now.'

Scowling, Douglas thumped off to the living-room, still bothered about the wealth of knowledge obtainable from adults lacking absolute proof. They were so *darn* right.

The house bell jangled.

Through the front door glass as he ran down the hall, Douglas saw a straw hat. He opened the door, irritated at the continuous again and again jangle of the bell.

'Good morning, child, is the lady of the house at home?'

Cold grey eyes in a long smooth walnut-coloured face, gazed upon him. The man was tall, thin, and carried a suitcase, a briefcase, an umbrella under one bent arm, gloves rich and thick and grey on his thin hands, and wore a horribly new straw hat.

Douglas backed up. 'She's busy.'

'I wish to rent her upstairs room, as advertised.'

'We've got ten boarders in the house, and it's already rented, go away.'

'Douglas!' Grandma was behind him suddenly, forging along the hall. 'How do you do?' she said to the stranger. 'Won't you step in? Go right on upstairs. Never mind this child.'

'Quite all right.' Unsmiling, the man stepped stiffly in. Douglas watched them ascend out of sight, heard Grandma detailing the conveniences of the upstairs room. A suitcase bumped down on the upstairs floor, and soon Grandma hurried down to take linens from the linen-closet, pile them on Douglas and send him scurrying up to the newly rented room.

Douglas paused at the room's threshold. It was transformed simply by the man being in the room a moment. The straw hat lay on the bed, the umbrella leaned stiff against one wall like a dead bat with dark wings tucked. Douglas blinked at the umbrella. The man stood in the centre of the room, his suitcase at his feet.

'Here.' Douglas decorated the bed with linens. 'We eat at twelve sharp and if you don't come down the soup'll get cold. Grandma fixes it so it will, every time.'

The man counted out ten pennies, tinkled them into Douglas's blouse pocket. 'We shall be friends,' he said.

It was funny, the man having nothing but pennies. Lots of them. No silver at all, no dimes, no quarters. Just new copper pennies.

Douglas thanked him. 'I'll drop these in my dime bank when I get them changed into a dime.'

'Saving money, young fellow?'

'Got six dollars and fifty cents. This makes sixty cents. For my camp trip in August.'

'I must wash now,' said the tall, strange man.

Once, at midnight, Douglas had awakened to hear a storm rumbling outside, the cold hard wind shaking the house, the rain driving against the windows. And then, a bolt of lightning had landed outside the window with a silent, terrific pounding. He remembered that fear. That fear of looking around at his room, seeing it strange and terrible in the instantaneous light.

It was the same, now, in this room. He stood looking at the stranger. This room was no longer the same, but changed indefinably, because this man, as quick as a lightning bolt, had shed his light about it. Douglas did not like it.

The door closed in his face.

The wooden fork came down, went up with mashed potatoes. Mr Koberman, for that was his name, had brought the fork and the wooden knife and spoon with him when Grandma called lunch.

'Mrs Spaulding,' he had said, quietly. 'My own cutlery; please use it. I will have lunch today, but from tomorrow on, only breakfast and supper.'

Grandma bustled in and out, bearing steaming tureens of soup and beans and mashed potatoes to impress her new boarder, while Douglas sat rattling his silverware on his plate, because he had discovered it irritated Mr Koberman.

'I know a trick,' said Douglas. 'Watch.' He picked a fork tine with his fingernail. He pointed at various sectors of the table, like a magician. Wherever he pointed, the sound of the vibrating fork-tine emerged, like a metal elfin voice. Simply done, of course. He simply pressed the fork handle on the table-top, secretly. The vibration came from the wood like a sounding board. It looked like magic. 'There, *there, and there!*' exclaimed Douglas, happily plucking the fork again. He pointed at Mr Koberman's soup and the noise came from it.

Mr Koberman's walnut-coloured face was hard and firm and awful. He pushed the soup bowl away, his lips twisting, and fell back in his chair.

Grandma appeared.

'Why, what's wrong, Mr Koberman?'

'I cannot eat the soup,' he said.

'Why?'

Mr Koberman glared at Douglas.

'Because I am full and can eat no more. Thank you.'

'Excusing himself, Mr Koberman walked upstairs.

'What did you do, just then?' asked Grandma at Douglas, sharply.

'Nothing, Grammy, why does he eat with wooden spoons?'

'You're not to question! When do you go back to school, anyway?'

'Seven weeks.'

'Oh, my land,' said Grandma.

*

Half-way to the second floor was a large, sun-filled window. It was framed by six-inch panes of orange, purple, blue, red and green glass. Some panes were yellow, some a wondrous burgundy.

In the enchanted late afternoons, when the sun fell through to strike upon the landing and slide down the stair banister, Douglas stood entranced by this window, peering at the world through the multi-coloured panes.

Now a blue world. Douglas pressed his nostrils against the blue pane, saw the blue-blue sky, the blue people and the blue street-cars and the trotting blue dogs.

Now—he shifted panes—there was an amber world. Two lemonish women glided by, looking like daughters of Fu Manchu. Douglas giggled. This pane made even the sunlight more purely golden, like taffy spilled on everything.

Douglas heard a noise above him. He knew Mr Koberman stood outside his door, watching.

Not turning, Douglas observed. 'All kinds of worlds. Blue ones, red ones, yellow ones. All different.'

After a long pause, Mr Koberman said, distractedly: 'That is true. All kinds of worlds. Yes. All different.'

The door closed. The hall was empty. Mr Koberman had gone in.

Douglas shrugged and found a new pane. 'Oh! Everything's *pink!*'

It was simple as a rain drop. Spooning his morning cereal, Douglas felt a simple, pure white flame of hatred stand inside him, burning with a steady, unflickering beauty. Upstairs, this morning, Mr Koberman's door had been ajar, the room empty. He had looked in, with distaste.

It was Mr Koberman's room now. Once it had been bright and flowery when Miss Sadlowe had lived there; full of nasturtiums and bright bolls of knitting cotton, bright pictures on the walls. When Mr Caples had lived there it reflected him: his athletic vivacity, his tennis shoes on a chair, a disembodied sweater crumpled on the bed, wrinkled pants in the closet, cut-outs of pretty girls on the bureau. But, now . . .

Now the room was Koberman Land. Bare and clean and cold and everything microscopically set in place. Not a microbe or dust-mote or oxygen cell existed in the room without having an appointed and irrevocable station.

Douglas finished breakfast, feeding simultaneously on one part buttered toast, two parts hatred.

He walked up to the landing and stared out of the coloured glasses.

Mr Koberman strolled by below, on the sidewalk, on his morning exercise. He walked straight, cane looped on arm half-way to elbow, his straw hat glued to his head with patent oil.

Mr Koberman was a blue man walking through a blue world with blue trees and blue flowers and— something else.

There was something about Mr Koberman. Douglas squinted. The blue glass *did* things to Mr Koberman. His face, his suit—

There was no time to fathom it. Mr Koberman glanced up just then, saw Douglas, and raised his cane-umbrella as if to strike, then put it down swiftly and hurried to the front door.

'Young man,' he said, coming up the stairs, 'what were you doing?'

'Just looking.'

'That's all, it is?'

'Yes, sir.'

Mr Koberman stood, fighting himself. The veins stood out on his face like small, grey wires. His eyes were deep black holes.

Saying nothing, he went downstairs for another walk around the block.

Douglas played in his sand-box in the backyard for half an hour. At about nine-thirty he heard the crash and the shattering tinkle. He jumped up. He heard Grandma's slippers scuffing in the hall, hurriedly, then scuffing back to the kitchen. The screen door *swannged* open, on its wire spring restrainer.

'Douglas!'

She held the old razor strop in her hand.

'I told you time and again never to fling your basketball against the house! Oh, I could just cry!'

'I been sitting right here,' he protested.

'Come in here! See what you done!'

The great coloured window panes were tumbled in a rainbow chaos on the upstairs landing. The basketball lay on the ruins.

Before Douglas could even begin telling his innocence, Grandma struck him seven stinging whops on his rump. Screaming, Douglas leaped like a fish, and wherever he landed he was whopped again! He sang an age-old song to his wild dancing.

Much later, hiding his mind in a pile of sand in the

sand-box, like an ostrich, Douglas nursed his pain.
He knew who'd thrown that basketball to shatter the
coloured windows. A man with a straw hat and a stiff
umbrella, and a cold, grey room. Yeah, yeah, yeah.
He dribbled tears in the sand. Just wait. Just wait.

The thin, tinkling shuf-shuf-shuf noise was
Grandma sweeping up the glittering debris. She
brought it out back and cascaded it into the trash-bin.
Blue, pink, white, yellow meteors of glass dropped
brightly down. Grandma looked broken-hearted.

When she was gone, Douglas dragged himself over
to save out three pieces of the precious glass; pink
and green and blue. He had an idea why Mr Koberman disliked the coloured windows. These—he
clinked them in his fingers—would be worth saving.

Mr Koberman worked nights and slept all day. Each
morning at eight he arrived home, devoured a light
breakfast, took a brief walk around the block, then
climbed primly upstairs to sleep soundlessly through-
out the day until six at night, when he came down
to the huge supper with all the other boarders.

Mr Koberman's sleeping habits made it necessary
for Douglas to be quiet. Not being quiet by nature,
frustration set in on him like a growing abscess.

Resultantly, when Grandma visited next door at
Mrs Eddy's or bought groceries at Mrs Singer's, Douglas would vent his repressions by stomping up and
down the stairs beating upon a drum. Golf-balls,
rolled slowly down the steps, were also delightful.
Followed by a quick shuttling of the house killing
Indians and flushing all the toilets three times in
succession.

After three days, Douglas realised he was getting no complaints. On the fourth day, after Grandma was gone to the store, he yelled outside Mr Koberman's door ten minutes straight, without criticism. Then, and only then, did he dare to try the door, carefully, and open it.

The room was in half-light, the shades drawn. Mr Koberman lay on top of the covers of his bed, in sleeping clothes, breathing gently, up and down. He didn't move. His face was motionless.

'Hello, Mr Koberman.'

The colourless walls echoed the man's regular breathing.

'Mr Koberman, hello!'

Bouncing the golf-ball, Douglas advanced. No response. He yelled. Still no answer. Mr Koberman lay like a papier-mâché dummy, not complaining, his eyes shut.

'Mr Koberman!'

Douglas searched the room with quick eyes. On the bureau rested the wooden eating utensils. This gave Douglas an idea. He ran and got a silver fork, came back. Picking the tines he held it close to the sleeping face.

Mr Koberman winced. He twisted on his bed, groaning, muttering bitterly.

Response. Good. Swell.

Another ting of the fork. Mr Koberman twitched in a nightmare of vibrations, but could not wake up. He didn't look as if he could, even if he wanted to.

Douglas remembered about the coloured glass. He drew a pink shard from his pocket and stared through it at Mr Koberman.

The clothes dissolved off of Mr Koberman. The pink glass had something to do with it. Or maybe it was the clothes themselves, being *on* Mr Koberman. Douglas licked his lips. He could see *inside* Mr Koberman.

Mr Koberman was—weird inside.

Very weird. Very interesting.

He was beginning to enjoy himself when the front door banged. Grandma was home.

Douglas had to come downstairs, frustrated, trying to look innocent.

When a slow heavy tread filled the hall, and a thick mahogany cane thumped in the cane-rack, that always meant Grandfather was home for the day. He arrived from his newspaper office each night, shortly ahead of the boarders, at five-fifteen, a copy of his own newspaper folded into his black coat-pocket along with a pink peppermint stick to be used expressly for spoiling Douglas' dinner-appetite.

Douglas ran to embrace the large stomach that was Grandpa's main defence against a vigorously long life-battle with circumstance. Grandpa, peering down over the cliff of that stomach, cried, 'Hello, down there!'

Seated in the great Morris chair, his spectacles attached, Grandpa scanned the paper with a keen eye.

'Grandma cut chickens again today. It's fun watching,' said Douglas.

Grandpa kept reading. 'Chickens? Again? That's twice this week. She's the chickenest woman. You like to watch her cut 'em, eh? Cold-blooded little pepper, Ha!'

Douglas felt the subterranean laughter explode down through the huge old bones, echo out on Grandpa's vibrant knee-cap.

'I'm just curious,' said Douglas.

'You *are*,' rumbled Grandpa, pursing his lips, scowling. 'I remember that day when the young lady was killed at the rail station. Didn't bother you a mite. You just walked over and looked at her, blood and all.'

'But, why shouldn't I look?'

'Doesn't it make you sick?' Grandpa put the paper aside.

'No.'

'Queer duck. Sensible, though. Stay that way, Dougie-boy. Fear nothing, ever in life. Life's full of things not worth fearing. Bodies are bodies and blood is blood. The only bad things are those we make in our minds. We teach each other fear. We learn certain reactions to certain stimuli. Death, for instance. Orientals deem it fairly fine and honourable to die. But some European cultures have trumped up sassafras about death being a dark horror. Why—'

He stopped, blinked, swallowed, and laughed.

'What *am* I saying? You don't understand one word—'

'Sure I do. Go ahead, Gramps. It's fun.'

'Funny duck. Your father raised you funny. But then, him being a military man, and you so close to him 'till you come here last year.'

'I'm not funny. I'm just *me*.'

'There—' Grandpa nodded, 'you *have* a point! There's no norm among humans, not really. Certain cultural norms, perhaps, but individual norms, no, no.'

This seemed like the moment ripened on the tree of time for picking. Douglas picked.

'Gramps, what if a man didn't have no heart, lungs or stomach?'

Grandpa was used to such questions. 'Why, then, I guess he'd be dead.'

'No, I don't mean that. I mean, what if he didn't have a heart or no lungs or no stomach but still walked around? Alive.'

'That,' rumbled Gramps, 'would be a miracle.'

'Besides,' said Douglas, swiftly. 'I don't mean a— a miracle. I mean—what if he was all *different* inside? Not like me.'

'Oh, I see. Umm. Well, he wouldn't be quite human then, would he, boy?'

'I guess not.' Douglas stared at the watch-fobbed stomach. 'Gramps. Gramps, you got a heart and a brain and lungs, Gramps?'

'I should live to tell you!'

'How do you *know*?'

'Uh—' Gramps stopped. 'Well.' He had to laugh. 'Tell the truth, I don't know. Never seen them. Never been to a doctor, never had an x-ray. Might as well be potato-solid for all I know.'

'How about me? Have *I* got a stomach?'

'You certainly *have*!' said Grandma, in the parlour entrance. ' 'Cause I feed it. And you've lungs, because you scream loud enough to wake the crumblees. And you've dirty hands, go wash them! Dinner's ready. Grandpa, come on. Douglas, git!'

She tinkled a little black lacquered metal bell in the hall.

In the rush of boarders streaming downstairs,

Grandpa, if he had intentions of questioning Douglas further about the weird conversation, lost his opportunity. If dinner delayed an instant more, Grandma and the potatoes would develop simultaneous lumps.

The other boarders, laughing and talking at the table, Mr Koberman silent and sullen between them—this attitude being attributed to liver trouble by Grandma—were put into a silent stasis by Grandfather who cleared his throat and spoke about the recent deaths in the town.

'Save that for later, when we drink our coffee,' said Grandma.

'It's certainly enough to make a newspaper editor prick up his ancient ears,' said Grandpa, carefully eyeing them all. 'That young Miss Larsson, lived over across the ravine, now. Found her dead three days ago for no reason, just funny kinds of tattoos all over her, and a facial expression would make Dante cringe. And that other young lady, what was her name? Whitely? She disappeared and never did come back.'

'Those things happen alla time,' said Mr Peters, the garage mechanic, chewing. 'Ever peek in the Missing People's Bureau file? It's *that* long.' He illustrated. 'Can't tell *what* happens to most of 'em.'

Grandma cut in. 'Anyone want more dressing?' She ladled liberal portions from the chicken's sad interior. Douglas watched, thinking about how that chicken had had two kinds of guts—God-made and Man-made.

Well, how about *three* kinds of guts?
Eh?

Why not?

Conversation continued merry about the mysterious death of so-and-so, and, oh yes, remember a week ago, Marion Barsumian died of heart failure, but maybe that didn't connect up, or did it, you're crazy, forget it, why talk about it at supper, on a full stomach? So.

Cigarettes fired, the diners idled lazily into the parlour, where Grandpa let somebody interrupt him on occasion when he needed breath.

'Never can tell,' said the garage mechanic. 'Maybe we got a vampire in town.'

'In the year 1927? Oh, go on now.'

'Sure. Kill 'em with silver bullets. Anything silver for that matter. I read it in a book somewhere, once. Sure, I did.'

Douglas sat on the floor looking up at Mr Koberman who ate with wooden knives and forks and spoons, and carried only copper pennies in his pocket.

'It'd be poor judgement,' said Grandpa, 'to call anything by a name. We don't even know what a hobgoblin or a vampire or a troll is. Could be a lot of things. You can't heave them into categories with labels, and say they'll act one way or another. That'd be silly. They're people, people who do things. Yes, that's the way to put it—people who *do* things.'

'Good evening, everyone,' said Mr Koberman, and got up and went out for his evening walk to work.

The radio was turned on. Card games were played. Ice cream was bought and served later. Then, the goodnights, and into bed.

*

The stars, the moon, the wind, the clock ticking and the chiming of hours into dawn, the sun coming up, and here it was another morning, another day, and Mr Koberman coming from his walk after breakfast. Douglas stood off like a small mechanism whirring and watching with carefully microscopic eyes.

At noon, Grandma went to the store to buy groceries.

Douglas yelled outside Mr Koberman's door for a minute, and then tried to enter. This time the door was locked. He had to run and get the pass-key.

Clutching the pass-key, and the pieces of coloured glass nervously, he entered and closed the door and heard Mr Koberman breathing deep. Douglas placed the blue glass fragment over his own eyes.

Looking through it, he found himself in a blue room, in a blue world different from the world he knew. As different as was the red world. Aquamarine furniture, cobalt bed-clothes, turquoise ceilings, and the sullen dark blue of Mr Koberman's face and arms, and his blue chest rising, falling. Also—something else.

Mr Koberman's eyes were wide open, staring at him with a hungry darkness. Douglas fell back, pulled the blue glass from his face. Mr Koberman's eyes were shut. Blue glass again—open. Blue glass away— shut. Blue glass again—open. Away—shut. Funny. Douglas experimented, trembling. Through the glass the eyes seemed to peer hungrily, avidly through the closed lids, like little flashlights. Without the blue glass they seemed tight shut.

But it was the rest of Mr Koberman's body . . .

Douglas must have stood amazed for five minutes.

Thinking about blue worlds, red worlds, yellow worlds, side by side, living together like glass panes around the big white stair window. Side by side, the coloured panes, the different worlds; Mr Koberman had said so himself.

So this was why the windows had been broken. At least partially why.

'Mr Koberman, wake up!'

No response.

'Mr Koberman, where do you work at night? Mr Koberman, where do you work?'

A little breeze stirred the blue window shade.

'In a red world or a green world or a yellow one, Mr Koberman!'

Over everything was a blue glass silence.

'Wait there,' said Douglas.

He walked out of the room, walked downstairs to the kitchen and pulled open the great squeaking drawers where all the knives lay gleaming. He picked out the sharpest, biggest one. Very calmly he walked into the hall, climbed back up the stairs again, opened the door to Mr Koberman's room and closed it.

Grandma was busy fingering a pie-crust into a pan when Douglas entered the kitchen to put something on the table.

'Grandma, what's this?'

She glanced up briefly, over her glasses. 'I don't know.'

It was square, like a box, and elastic. It was bright orange in colour. It had four square tubes, coloured blue, attached to it. It smelled funny. Not good but yet not bad.

'Ever see anything like it, Grandma?'

'No.'

'That's what *I* thought.'

Douglas left it there, went out of the kitchen. Five minutes later he returned with something else. 'How about *this?*'

It resembled a bright pink linked chain with a purple triangle at one end.

'Don't bother me,' sniffed Grandma. 'It's only a chain.'

He went away. Next time he came with two hands full. A ring, a square, a pyramid, a rectangle—and other shapes. 'This isn't all. Lots more where this came from.'

Grandma said, 'Yes, yes,' in a far-off tone, very busy.

'You were wrong, Grandma.'

'About what?'

'About all people being the same inside.'

'Stop talking nonsense.'

'Where's my piggy-bank?' he asked.

'On the mantel.'

'Thanks.'

He tromped into the parlour, reached up for the piggy-bank.

Grandpa came home from the office at five-fifteen.

'Grandpa, come upstairs.'

'Sure, son. Why?'

'Something to show you. It's not nice. But it's interesting.'

Grandpa chuckled, followed his grandson's feet up to Mr Koberman's room.

'Grandma mustn't know about this; she wouldn't

like it,' said Douglas. He pushed the door wide. 'There.'

Grandfather gasped.

Douglas remembered the last scene all the rest of his life. Standing over the naked body, the coroner and his assistants. Grandma, downstairs, asking somebody, 'What's going on up there?' and Grandpa saying, shakily, 'I'll take Douglas away on a long vacation so he can forget this whole ghastly affair. Ghastly, ghastly affair!'

Douglas said, 'Why should it be bad? I don't see anything bad. I don't feel bad.'

The coroner shivered and said: 'Koberman's dead, all right.'

His assistant sweated. 'Did you see those *things* in the pan of water and in the wrapping paper?'

'Oh, My God, My God, yes, I saw them.'

'Christ.'

The coroner bent over Mr Koberman's body. 'This better be kept secret, boys. It wasn't murder. It was a mercy the boy acted. God knows what may have happened if he hadn't.'

'What was Koberman—a vampire? a monster?'

'Maybe. I don't know. I don't know anything. Something—not human.' The coroner moved his hands deftly over the suture.

Douglas was proud of his work. He'd gone to much trouble. He had watched Grandma carefully and remembered. Needle and thread and all. All in all, Mr Koberman was as neat a job as any chicken ever popped into hell by Grandma.

'I heard the boy say that Koberman *lived* even after

all those *things* were taken out of him. Kept on *living*. God.'

'Did the boy say that?'

'He did.'

'Then, what killed Koberman?'

The coroner drew a few strands of sewing thread from their bedding. 'This—' he said.

Sunlight blinked coldly off a half-revealed treasure trove; six dollars and seventy cents worth of silver dimes inside Mr Koberman's chest.

'I think Douglas made a wise investment,' said the coroner, sewing the flesh back up over the 'dressing' quickly.

* * *

RAY BRADBURY has probably written more stories about the terrors of childhood than any other writer in this book. He grew up in a small Midwest town of America, and many of his spooky exploits as a child have been retold in famous short stories like 'The Emissary', about a boy's favourite dog that returns from the dead, The Small Assassin' which shows how even the youngest infant is capable of killing its parents, and 'Let's Play "Poison"' in which a child-hating teacher stops a boys' game with fatal results. In a number of these stories—like 'The Man Upstairs'—the main character has the author's own middle name, Douglas. His best-selling novels, *The Martian Chronicles* and *Fahrenheit 451*, have been made into films, and several of his stories portraying children as monsters or horribly pathetic victims have been adapted by the famous EC Horror Comics. In some of Ray Bradbury's stories he suggests that it is almost better to die young than face the dreaded changes of adulthood and death, and this has not always made him popular with adults—but he will always be one of my favourite authors.

DEAD LANGUAGE MASTER

Joan Aiken

Pridd is a show-off and utter thick at school. He likes to barge into girls and put glue on their hair. He also loathes Mr Fletcher, the Latin teacher, who drifts silently around the school trying to catch out misbehaving children and using out-of-date slang that makes everyone laugh at him. But when Pridd plots a ghastly trick using the master's old dog, the events that follow in school for the animal, his owner and the boy go from being scary to downright terrifying.

*   *   *

Mr Fletcher taught us Latin. He was the shape of a domino. No, that's wrong, because he wasn't square; he looked as if he had been cut out of a domino. He had shape but no depth, you felt he could have slipped through the crack at the hinge of a door if he'd gone sideways. Though I daresay if he'd really been able to do that he would have made more use of the faculty; he was great on stealing quietly along a passage and then opening the door very fast to see what we were all up to; he used to drift about silently like an old ghost, but if you had a keen sense of smell you always had advance warning of his arrival because of the capsule of stale cigarette smoke that he moved about in. He smoked nonstop; he used a holder, but even so his fingers were yellow up to the knuckles and so were his teeth when he bared them in a horsegrin. He had dusty black hair that hung in a lank flop over his big square forehead, and his feet were enormous; they curved as he put them down like a duck's flippers, which, I suppose, was why he could move so quietly. Even his car was quiet; it was a huge old German thing, we used to call it his Strudel, gunmetal grey, and he kept it polished and serviced to the last degree. He loved that car. The way it whispered in and out of the school yard, it was a wonder he hadn't run anyone down yet, and everyone thought he would sooner or later, as he was very short-sighted and wouldn't wear glasses. If someone kicked up a disturbance at the back of the classroom he'd first screw up his eyes and stick his head out, so that he looked like a snake, weaving his head about to try and focus on the guy who was making the row; then he'd start slowly down the aisle, thrusting his face between each line of desks; I can tell you it was quite an unnerving performance.

He seemed ageless; I suppose he might have been in his sixties but you couldn't be sure. He used to go to Germany every holidays and he had this dog Heinkel, a Dachshund. Heinkel looked older than his master, he was wheezy and rheumaticky, blind in one eye and had a wooden leg; I'm not kidding, he'd had to have a front foot amputated for some reason, and had this little sort of stilt strapped on so that he could hobble slowly about, very dot and carry. He didn't bother much, though; sat in the car most of the time, dozing and waiting for the day's lessons to finish.

None of our lot cared greatly for Latin, we didn't see the point of it, so we didn't have much in common with old Fletcher. We thought he was a funny old coot, a total square—he used words like 'topping' and 'ripping' which he must have picked out of the *Boy's Own Paper* in the nineteen-tens. He was dead keen on his subject and would have taught it quite well if anyone had been interested; the only time you saw a wintry smile light up his yellow face was when he was pointing out the beauties of some construction in Livy or Horace. Personally I don't mind, if you've got to do a thing you might as well do it decently, but a lot of the guys thought he was a dead bore. That was as far as it went until Pridd arrived, and till Fletcher became our form master.

Pridd's father was the new manager of the new supermarket; the family had just come to live in the town. Pridd was a big lumping boy, pobby, with a small head perched on no neck, and small knowing Chinese eyes. He liked maths, but every other subject bored him; he used to sit at the back of the room reading Hotcha inside his exercise book or filing down a bit of brass curtain-rod to shoot peas through. He detested Latin; couldn't see the point of it.

'I'm going to help my dad in the shop as soon as I get out of here,' he said, 'so what the hell's the use of a lot of crummy Caesar and Virgil? Latin's a dead language, who cares about its flipping principal parts? Principal parts! I'll bet old Fletcher hasn't even—' and he added something obscene; Pridd was very foul-mouthed and thought himself highly witty, but personally I considered him an utter thick; he used to barge straight into girls on purpose with his ten stone of misdirected energy, specially if they were trying to carry home a bowl of custard or jelly they'd made in Dom. Sci. His favourite idea of a joke was flicking glue on to girls' hair or pouring a bottleful of ink into somebody's desk when they weren't looking.

It was Pridd who christened Fletcher the Dead Language Master. 'Look out, here's the DLM,' he'd call in a piercing whisper, just loud enough to be heard, as Fletcher creaked in. Somehow the name stuck; it seemed gloomily appropriate to the poor old boy.

When Fletcher became our form master we suddenly realised that, instead of seeing him three times a week in Latin periods, we were stuck with him nearly all the time. He used to drift round like a moth between periods to see what we were up to, and there was nearly always trouble.

'Nyaaah,' he always began his sentences. 'Nyaaah, Pridd, what are you doing up on that windowsill?' He had a nasal, croaking voice like some rusty old bird.

'Nothing, sir,' Pridd would answer innocently, dropping the paper waterbomb he'd just constructed on to some girl's head and sliding back into the room all in one movement.

'Nyaah I don't really think that's so, Pridd, I'm afraid that means another visit to the headmaster.'

Pridd scowled. We don't have beating at our school, the main punishment is Saturday detention, and after Fletcher had been with us for three weeks Pridd had piled up enough Saturdays to last him right through the term. This riled him, because on Saturdays he always put on a white overall and helped his dad in the shop, earning three or four quid a time.

'I'll get my own back on the old scouse, you wait and see if I don't,' he muttered.

He needn't have bothered. His mere presence in the class was revenge enough. From the day of his arrival our form began to go to pieces. Sometimes only the four guys in the front row were making any pretence of following the lesson; everyone else would be watching Pridd and snickering at his crazy antics.

'Fat woman going upstairs,' he'd say, puffing out each cheek alternately, squinting at us out of his mud-coloured slit eyes. He'd buy plastic balloons and blow them up into rude shapes, or pass round pictures, or tell stories, of which he had an endless supply; most of them were just stupid but a few were funny. If he couldn't think of anything else to do he'd pretend to accidentally knock all the books off his desk, or let fall the lid with an almighty crash, anything to create a distraction.

Most of the masters tolerated him to some degree, slapping him down when he really got them riled, but Fletcher frankly loathed him; the loathing was mutual, you could feel it between them, cold as liquid air. He really made Fletcher's life hell. The Latin lessons soon deteriorated into utter chaos; no one even tried to learn. You could hear the whistling and stamping and talk and laughter all the way along the passage. Fletcher began to look more and more wizened and yellow: scooped out and sunk in like some old vegetable marrow that's thrown out on the compost heap because it's past eating.

Funnily enough I forget what act of Pridd's it was that started the final build-up to crisis; maybe it was tying a black thread round Fletcher's inkwell and twitching it off his desk when he was translating; or it might have been the time when Pridd sawed half through the blackboard pegs so that the board crashed down on Fletcher's toe as soon as he started writing. Whatever the deed, it made Fletcher so mad that Saturday detention wasn't enough; he also cancelled Pridd's permission to see the Fenner-Giugliani fight, and sent back the money to Pridd's father, and gave the ticket to another boy.

Pridd was absolutely savage with rage and disappointment; he'd been dead set on going to that fight. The school had had early privilege tickets and it was now too late to get another for love or money; nobody liked Pridd enough to give up a ticket, though he went round offering large sums.

He began to plot revenge.

It was a tradition that Fletcher always took his form for a picnic to Butt Lake on the last Monday of the summer term, and at first Pridd had it planned that he'd somehow contrive to trip Fletcher and push him into the lake.

'I bet the old twat can't swim,' he said. 'Wouldn't it be a laugh to see him flapping about in the water, silly old goat? "Nyaah, save me, save me, oh, won't somebody please save me?"'

In the end, however, fate gave Pridd a different opportunity.

We were fooling about in the school yard early on Monday morning when we noticed a gaggle of boys round Fletcher's car, all staring in.

'Perhaps the old fool's left his wallet in the car,' Pridd said hopefully. 'Let's go and see.'

It wasn't a wallet, though. It was the dog, Heinkel,

stretched out limp and dead on the seat; he must have died of heart failure or old age almost as soon as his master had gone off and left him; not before it was time either, poor thing. Whenever my father saw him he used to say, 'That dog ought to be put to sleep.'

Pridd joined the group and stood staring at Heinkel with his hands in his pockets. Then he began to snigger.

'We can do something with this,' he said. 'This is luscious!' He tried the door handle.

Usually Fletcher locked his car doors but today he hadn't. Pridd leaned in and picked up the dog.

'Keep round me, you lot,' he said, 'we don't want anyone to see us. Oh, won't the old DLM be surprised!'

'Wotcher going to do, Priddy?' someone said.

'Wait and see,' he said. I think he wasn't sure yet himself, as a matter of fact.

Suddenly I felt fed up with the whole business. I waited by the door as they went nudging and giggling up the stairs to our classroom. I was still hanging about, reading the notices in the hall, which I'd read hundreds of times before, when the school secretary came out. Her name's Miss Figgins, we call her Fig, of course; she's not a bad old thing, grey-haired and dumpy and motherly.

She looked in the car window and said, 'Where's Heinkel? I promised to have him while Mr Fletcher's in hospital.'

'Hospital?' I said. 'Is he going to hospital?'

'Oh dear,' she said. 'Slipped out. Shouldn't have mentioned it—he doesn't want it talked about. Don't pass it on, Gant, there's a good boy. I know you can be sensible if you choose.'

'Okay,' I said. 'But you needn't bother about Heinkel, anyway. He's just died—the boys went to tell Mr Fletcher.'

'Oh dear,' she said, 'poor little thing. Mr Fletcher will be upset. Not but what it was time, I must say. Well I suppose I needn't trouble, then.'

When I got up to the classroom Fletcher had already arrived. He looked at me tiredly as I slid into my desk but didn't say anything. There was no sign of Heinkel, but the atmosphere in the room was electric; I looked about cautiously, wondering what Pridd had done with him. Then I noticed that everyone's attention was focused on the cupboard where Fletcher kept the books like Cicero and Ovid and Horace that weren't used every day; whenever Fletcher moved that way the tension in the class shot up a couple of degrees.

Fletcher wasn't getting out any books yet, though; he was returning homework, making sharp remarks as he passed each exercise book back to its owner.

When he'd returned the last one he cleared his throat and addressed the whole form.

'Nyaaah! Attention, please. Attention!'

Pridd muttered something to his neighbour and a line of giggles shot along the back row like fire through dry grass. Someone spluttered, someone else coughed, and in a moment half the class were rocking about in hysterics, paying no attention to what Fletcher was trying to say.

I noticed Fletcher's hands were trembling. He looked about him two or three times, hurriedly, as if he hardly knew what he wanted, then snatched up the poker from the stove and banged on his table twice.

'Attention! I *will* have attention when I speak!'

A sort of silence fell. Only at the back Pridd was heard to mutter, 'Dopey old nana,' and someone let out a suppressed titter.

'Pridd!' Fletcher shouted. His chest heaved. He clutched the poker and started to step forward. We all waited breathlessly, wondering if Pridd had really gone too far this time and if Fletcher was going to bash him. But he didn't. He wiped his forehead with the back of his other hand and said.

'I'm not going to give you a lesson today. I'm not going to teach you any more. I'm leaving.'

'Hooray,' somebody muttered, just audibly.

'I'm leaving,' Fletcher said, raising his voice. 'And if you want to know why, it's because of you. It's because you've made my life an utter misery these last few terms with your stupid, senseless insubordination and your idiocy and your *malevolence.* You used to be a decent enough lot of boys. I don't know what's come over you. I really don't. All I can say is, I'm sorry for the next man who tries to teach you Latin. You've finished me, and I hope you're proud of yourselves.'

He stared at us, trembling, and we stared back at him. There were beads of sweat on his yellow forehead. He noticed he was still holding the poker and threw it down.

'I shan't be taking you on the usual picnic,' he said. 'Frankly, I've no wish to. Mr Whitney will take you instead. Gant, you're head boy; here's ten pounds, you can buy some food with it.'

'Oh gosh, thank you, sir,' I said. I didn't want to take it but he pushed it at me and went on speaking.

'I only hope that some day you'll come to understand the amount of suffering you caused. Maybe then you'll learn to behave like civilised human beings. That's all.'

He turned and walked out of the door. Thunderstruck, we gaped after him. Then Pridd exclaimed,

'Christ, we've got to get the dog back into the car somehow!'

'Why?' someone said.

'Why, you nut? We don't want the dog in the cupboard for the next term, do we? Come on, pretend to take the old goat's Latin books down.'

Fletcher was just getting into his car when half the class hurtled into the yard. He didn't seem worried about Heinkel—evidently assumed Miss Figgins had taken him. He gave us a short unsmiling look.

'What is it?'

'We just came down to say goodbye, sir, and thanks for the money,' Pridd said unctuously. 'You forgot your books, sir. Shall we put them in the boot?'

'You needn't have bothered—I shan't want them again.' But Fletcher pressed the button that opened the luggage compartment. The flap swung back and down. Two or three boys clustered by the driving window and two or three more stood round Pridd as he took Heinkel from under his blazer. He sat his fat bottom on the lid and leaned far in, to stow the dog's body right at the back of the compartment. He was grinning again, his Chinese eyes were like slits, and it was plain that he was relishing the thought of

Fletcher's actions when he opened up to get out the books.

Fletcher started the engine and glanced into his rear-view mirror.

I'm not sure how it happened; evidently Fletcher couldn't see Pridd's head in the mirror, for he pressed the button to shut the boot. The flap swung up, Pridd hastily and instinctively pulled his legs in, and, hey, presto! the boot was shut and he was inside it. Fletcher released the handbrake and the car shot silently forward, across the yard and out of the gate.

Somebody shouted, somebody waved frantically. But Fletcher took no notice—I suppose he thought we were just waving a ribald goodbye. Or did he *know* he had Pridd with him?

We shall never learn the answer to that, because Fletcher wasn't seen again. He didn't go to hospital. His car was found five days later, on a lonely stretch of coast, with Fletcher's clothes in a neat, folded pile on the driver's seat. Otherwise the car was empty, except for the contents of the boot.

*   *   *

JOAN AIKEN is well known for her fantasy and thriller stories for children, among them a famous sequence of novels describing an alternative history of England, which begins with *The Wolves of Willoughby Chase*. As well as many adult novels, she has produced a wealth of short stories for children, often featuring young boys and girls in peril. Among her collections of these are *The Green Flash* and *A Bundle of Nerves* and, most recently, *A Creepy Company*.

Joan Aiken is the daughter of the American writer, Conrad Aiken, who wrote the classic short story 'Silent Snow, Secret Snow'. She lives in Rye in Sussex, near the former home of the novelist Henry James, author of the famous supernatural novel, *The Turn of the Screw*. One of her adult novels is actually about a haunting at this house, now a popular tourist attraction.

HERE THERE BE TYGERS

Stephen King

Charles always gets nervous when he needs to use the toilet at school. It's not just that his teacher, Miss Bird, always embarrasses him in front of all the other kids in the class when he asks to go, or even that the bullying Kenny Griffen gives him a hard time and makes him look small in the eyes of pretty Cathy Scott. No, there is another, far more scary reason altogether—and it is to do with the something that lurks in the school basement . . . waiting.

*   *   *

Charles needed to go the bathroom very badly.

There was no longer any use in trying to fool himself that he could wait for recess. His bladder was screaming at him, and Miss Bird had caught him squirming.

There were three third-grade teachers in the Acorn Street Grammar School. Miss Kinney was young and blonde and bouncy and had a boyfriend who picked her up after school in a blue Camaro. Mrs Trask was shaped like a Moorish pillow and did her hair in braids and laughed boomingly. And there was Miss Bird.

Charles had known he would end up with Miss Bird. He had *known* that. It had been inevitable.

Because Miss Bird obviously wanted to destroy him. She did not allow children to go to the basement. The basement, Miss Bird said, was where the boilers were kept, and well-groomed ladies and gentlemen would never go down *there*, because basements were nasty, sooty old things. Young ladies and gentlemen do not go to the basement, she said. They go to the *bathroom.*

Charles squirmed again.

Miss Bird cocked an eye at him. 'Charles,' she said clearly, still pointing her pointer at Bolivia, 'do you need to go to the bathroom?'

Cathy Scott in the seat ahead of him giggled, wisely covering her mouth.

Kenny Griffen sniggered and kicked Charles under his desk.

Charles went bright red.

'Speak up, Charles,' Miss Bird said brightly. 'Do you need to—'

(*urinate she'll say urinate she always does*)

'Yes, Miss Bird.'

'Yes, what?'

'I have to go to the base—to the bathroom.'

Miss Bird smiled. 'Very well, Charles. You may go to the bathroom and urinate. Is that what you need to do? Urinate?'

Charles hung his head, convicted.

'Very well, Charles. You may do so. And next time kindly don't wait to be asked.'

General giggles. Miss Bird rapped the board with her pointer.

Charles trudged up the row towards the door, thirty pairs of eyes boring into his back, and every one of those kids, including Cathy Scott, knew that he was going into the bathroom to urinate. The door was at least a football field's length away. Miss Bird did not go on with the lesson but kept her silence until he had opened the door, entered the blessedly empty hall, and shut the door again.

He walked down towards the boys' bathroom

(*basement basement basement IF I WANT*)

dragging his fingers along the cool tile of the wall, letting them bounce over the thumbtack-stippled bulletin board and slide lightly across the red

(*BREAK GLASS IN CASE OF EMERGENCY*)

fire-alarm box.

Miss Bird *liked* it. Miss Bird *liked* making him have a red face. In front of Cathy Scott—who *never* needed to go to the basement, was that fair?—and everybody else.

Old b-i-t-c-h, he thought. He spelled because he had decided last year God didn't say it was a sin if you spelled.

He went into the boys' bathroom.

It was very cool inside, with a faint, not unpleasant smell of chlorine hanging pungently in the air. Now, in the middle of the morning, it was clean and deserted, peaceful and quite pleasant, not at all like the smoky, stinky cubicle at the Star Theatre downtown.

The bathroom

(!*basement*!)

was built like an L, the short side lined with tiny square mirrors and white porcelain washbowls and a paper towel dispenser,

(NIBROC).

the longer side with two urinals and three toilet cubicles.

Charles went around the corner after glancing morosely at his thin, rather pallid face in one of the mirrors.

The tiger was lying down at the far end, just underneath the pebbly-white window. It was a large tiger, with tawny venetian blinds and dark stripes laid across its pelt. It looked up alertly at Charles, and its green eyes narrowed. A kind of silky, purring grunt issued from its mouth. Smooth muscles flexed, and the tiger got to its feet. Its tail switched, making little chinking sounds against the porcelain side of the last urinal.

The tiger looked quite hungry and very vicious.

Charles hurried back the way he had come. The door seemed to take forever to wheeze pneumatically closed behind him, but when it did, he considered himself safe. This door only swung in, and he could not remember ever reading or hearing that tigers are smart enough to open doors.

Charles wiped the back of his hand across his nose. His heart was thumping so hard he could hear it. He still needed to go to the basement, worse than ever.

He squirmed, winced, and pressed a hand against his belly. He *really* had to go to the basement. If he could only be sure no one would come, he could use the girls'. It was right across the hall. Charles looked at it longingly, knowing he would never dare, not in a million years. What if Cathy Scott should come? Or—black horror!—what if *Miss Bird* should come?

Perhaps he had imagined the tiger.

He opened the door wide enough for one eye and peeked in.

The tiger was peeking back from around the angle of the L, its eye a sparkling green. Charles fancied he could see a tiny blue fleck in that deep brilliance, as if the tiger's eye had eaten one of his own. As if—

A hand slid around his neck.

Charles gave a stifled cry and felt his heart and stomach cram up into his throat. For one terrible moment he thought he was going to wet himself.

It was Kenny Griffen, smiling complacently. 'Miss Bird sent me after you 'cause you been gone six years. You're in trouble.'

'Yeah, but I can't go to the basement,' Charles said, feeling faint with the fright Kenny had given him.

'Yer constipated!' Kenny chortled gleefully. 'Wait'll I tell *Caaathy!*'

'You better not!' Charles said urgently. 'Besides, I'm not. There's a tiger in there.'

'What's he doing?' Kenny asked. 'Taking a piss?'

'I don't know,' Charles said, turning his face to the wall. 'I just wish he'd go away.' He began to weep.

'Hey,' Kenny said, bewildered and a little frightened. 'Hey.'

'What if I *have* to go? What if I can't help it? Miss Bird'll say—'

'Come on,' Kenny said, grabbing his arm in one hand and pushing the door open with the other. 'You're making it up.'

They were inside before Charles, terrified, could break free and cower back against the door.

'Tiger,' Kenny said disgustedly. 'Boy, Miss Bird's gonna *kill* you.'

'It's around the other side.'

Kenny began to walk past the washbowls. 'Kitty-kitty-kitty? Kitty?'

'Don't!' Charles hissed.

Kenny disappeared around the corner. 'Kitty-kitty? Kitty-kitty? Kit—'

Charles darted out the door again and pressed himself against the wall, waiting, his hands over his mouth and his eyes squinched shut, waiting, waiting for the scream.

There was no scream.

He had no idea how long he stood there, frozen, his bladder bursting. He looked at the door to the boys' basement. It told him nothing. It was just a door.

He wouldn't.

He *couldn't.*

But at last he went in.

The washbowls and the mirrors were neat, and the faint smell of chlorine was unchanged. But there seemed to be a smell under it. A faint, unpleasant smell, like freshly sheared copper.

With groaning (but silent) trepidation, he went to the corner of the L and peeped around.

The tiger was sprawled on the floor, licking its large paws with a long pink tongue. It looked incuriously at Charles. There was a torn piece of shirt caught in one set of claws.

But his need was a white agony now, and he couldn't help it. He *had* to. Charles tiptoed back to the white porcelain basin closest the door.

Miss Bird slammed in just as he was zipping his pants.

'Why, you dirty, filthy little boy,' she said almost reflectively.

Charles was keeping a weather eye on the corner. 'I'm sorry, Miss Bird ... the tiger ... I'm going to clean the sink ... I'll use soap ... I swear I will ...'

'Where's Kenneth?' Miss Bird asked calmly.

'I don't know.'

He didn't, really.

'Is he back there?'

'*No!*' Charles cried.

Miss Bird stalked to the place where the room bent. 'Come here, Kenneth. Right this moment.'

'Miss Bird—'

But Miss Bird was already around the corner. She meant to pounce. Charles thought Miss Bird was about to find out what pouncing was really all about.

He went out the door again. He got a drink at the drinking fountain. He looked at the American flag hanging over the entrance to the gym. He looked at the bulletin board. Woodsy Owl said GIVE A HOOT, DON'T POLLUTE. Officer Friendly said NEVER RIDE WITH STRANGERS. Charles read everything twice.

Then he went back to the classroom, walked down his row to his seat with his eyes on the floor, and slid into his seat. It was a quarter to eleven. He took out *Roads to Everywhere* and began to read about Bill at the Rodeo.

*   *   *

STEPHEN KING is probably the world's top-selling author of horror novels and has had most of his best-selling books like *Carrie*, *The Shining* and *Firestarter* made into films. As a child he loved reading mystery stories, and while he was at the University of

Maine he wrote a column in the school paper called 'King's Garbage Truck' about horror films, television and books. In 1956 he published his first story, 'I Was a Teenage Graverobber'. He was a teacher of English in Maine before creating a sensation with his first novel, *Carrie*. Since that he has become an international best-seller with his books selling millions of copies in dozens of languages. Children—especially teenagers—appear in a lot of his novels and short stories, and while some have consciences about what they do, many of the others are just plain evil and use their powers against kids and adults with terrible effect. Stephen King has promised that there will be lots more stories like the one you have just read about the scary world of childhood.

THE TRICK

Ramsey Campbell

Debbie isn't frightened of Hallowe'en or of the old woman who lives opposite, Miss Trodden. Some people say she is a witch and certainly she stays indoors most of the time, just peering out and occasionally shouting at the children playing for making too much noise. Most of the adults in the street avoid her, and she seems to frighten animals, too. So why should the old lady suddenly warn Debbie and her friend, Sandra, to stay away from the scary old disused tunnel where a little boy had once run and never been seen again?

*   *   *

As October waned Debbie forgot about the old witch; she didn't associate her with Hallowe'en. Hallowe'en wasn't frightening. After the long depression following the summer holidays, it was the first night of the winter excitements: not as good as Guy Fawkes' Night or Christmas, but still capable of excluding less pleasant things from Debbie's mind—the sarcastic teacher, the gangs of boys who leaned against the shops, the old witch.

Debbie wasn't really frightened of her, not at her age. Even years ago, when Debbie was a little kid, she hadn't found her terrifying. Not like some things:

not like her feverish night when the dark in her bed-room had grown like mould on the furniture, making the familiar chair and wardrobe soft and huge. Nor like the face that had looked in her bedroom window once, when she was ill: a face like a wrinkled monkey's, whose jaw drooped as if melting, lower and lower; a face that had spoken to her in a voice that sagged as the face did—a voice that must have been a car's engine struggling to start.

The witch had never seized Debbie with panic, as those moments had. Perhaps she was only an old woman, after all. She lived in a terraced house, in the row opposite Debbie's home. People owned their houses in that row, but Debbie's parents only rented the top half of a similar building. They didn't like the old woman; nobody did.

Whenever the children played outside her house she would come out to them. 'Can't you make your row somewhere else? Haven't you got a home to go to?' 'We're playing outside our own house,' someone might say. 'You don't own the street.' Then she would stand and stare at them, with eyes like grey marbles. The fixed lifeless gaze always made them uneasy; they would dawdle away, jeering.

Parents were never sympathetic. 'Play somewhere else, then,' Debbie's father would say. Her parents were more frightened of the witch than she was. 'Isn't her garden awful,' she'd once heard her mother say-ing. 'It makes the whole street look like a slum. But we mustn't say anything, we're only tenants.' Debbie thought that was just an excuse.

Why were they frightened? The woman was small, hardly taller than Debbie. Boys didn't like to play near her house in case they had to rescue a football, to grope through the slimy nets, tall as a child, of weeds and grass full of crawlers. But that was only nasty, not frightening. Debbie wasn't even sure why the woman was supposed to be a witch.

Perhaps it was her house. 'Keep away from my house,' she told nearby children when she went out, as though they would want to go near the drab unpainted crumbling house that was sinking into its own jungle. The windows were cracked and thick with grime; when the woman's face peered out it looked like something pale stirring in a dirty jar. Sometimes children stood outside shouting and screaming to make the face loom. Boys often dared each other to peer in, but rarely did. Perhaps that was it, then: her house looked like a witch's house. Sometimes black smoke that looked solid as oil dragged its long swollen body from the chimney.

There were other things. Animals disliked her almost as much as she disliked them. Older brothers said that she went out after midnight, hurrying through the mercury-vapour glare towards the derelict streets across the main road; but older brothers often made up stories. When Debbie tried to question her father he only told her not to be stupid. 'Who's been wasting your time with that?'

The uncertainty annoyed her. If the woman were a witch she must be in retirement; she didn't do anything. Much of the time—at least, during the day—she stayed in her house: rarely answering the door, and then only to peer through a crack and send the intruder away. What did she do, alone in the dark house? Sometimes people odder than herself would visit her: a tall thin woman with glittering wrists and eyes, who dressed in clothes like tapestries of lurid flame; two fat men, Tweedledum and Tweedledee draped in lethargically flapping black cloaks. They might be witches too.

'Maybe she doesn't want anyone to know she's a witch,' suggested Debbie's friend Sandra. Debbie didn't really care. The old woman only annoyed her, as bossy adults did. Besides, Hallowe'en was coming. Then, on Hallowe'en morning—just when Debbie had managed to forget her completely—the woman did the most annoying thing of all.

Debbie and Sandra had wheeled their prams to the supermarket, feeling grown-up. On the way they'd met Lucy, who never acted her age. When Lucy had asked, 'Where are you taking your dolls?' Sandra had replied loftily, 'We aren't taking our *dolls* anywhere.' She'd done the shopping each Saturday morning since she was nine, so that her mother could work. Often she shopped in the evenings, because her mother was tired after work, and then Debbie would accompany her, so that she felt less uneasy in the crowds beneath the white glare. This Saturday morning Debbie was shopping too.

The main road was full of crowds trying to beat the crowds. Boys sat like a row of shouting ornaments on the railing above the underpass; women queued a block for cauliflowers, babies struggled screaming in prams. The crowds flapped as a wind fumbled along the road. Debbie and Sandra manoeuvred their prams to the supermarket. A little girl was racing a trolley through the aisles, jumping on the back for a ride. How childish, Debbie thought.

When they emerged Sandra said, 'Let's walk to the tunnel and back.'

She couldn't be anxious to hurry home to vacuum the flat. They wheeled their laden prams towards the tunnel, which fascinated them. A railway cutting divided the streets a few hundred yards beyond the supermarket, in the derelict area. Houses crowded both its banks, their windows and doorways blinded and gagged with boards. From the cutting, disused railway lines probed into a tunnel beneath the main road—and never reappeared, so far as Debbie could see.

The girls pushed their prams down an alley, to the near edge of the cutting. Beside them the remains of back yards were cluttered with fragments of brick. The cutting was rather frightening, in a delicious way. Rusty metal skeletons sat tangled unidentifiably among the lines, soggy cartons flapped sluggishly, a door lay as though it led to something in the soil. Green sprouted minutely between scatterings of rubble.

Debbie stared down at the tunnel, at the way it burrowed into the dark beneath the earth. Within the mouth was only a shallow rim, surrounding thick darkness. No: now she strained her eyes she made out a further arch of dimmer brick, cut short by the dark. As she peered another formed, composed as much of darkness as of brick. Beyond it she thought something pale moved. The surrounding daylight flickered with Debbie's peering; she felt as though she were being drawn slowly into the tunnel. What was it, the pale feeble stirring? She held on to a broken wall, so as to lean out to peer; but a voice startled her away.

'Go on. Keep away from there.' It was the old witch, shouting from the main road, just as if they were little kids. To Debbie she looked silly: her head poked over the wall above the tunnel, as if someone had put a turnip there to grimace at them.

'We're all right,' Sandra called impatiently. 'We know what we're doing.' They wouldn't have gone too near the cutting; years ago a little boy had run into the tunnel and had never been seen again.

'Just do as you're told. Get away.' The head hung above the wall, staring hatefully at them, looking even more like a turnip.

'Oh, let's go home,' Debbie said. 'I don't want to stay here now, anyway.'

They wheeled their prams around the chunks that littered the street. At the main road the witch was waiting for them. Her face frowned, glaring from its perch above the small black tent of her coat. Little more of her was visible; scuffed black snouts poked from beneath the coat, hands lurked in her drooping sleeves; one finger was hooked around the cane of a tattered umbrella. 'And keep away from there in future,' she said harshly.

'Why, is that your house?' Debbie muttered.

'That's where she keeps her bats' eyes.'

'What's that?' The woman's grey eyebrows writhed up, threatening. Her head looked like an old apple, Debbie thought, with mould for eyebrows and tufts of dead grass stuck on top. 'What did you just say?' the woman shouted.

She was repeating herself into a fury when she was interrupted. Debbie tried not to laugh. Sandra's dog Mop was the interruption; he must have jumped out of Sandra's back yard. He was something like a stumpy-legged terrier, black and white and spiky. Debbie liked him, even though he'd once run away with her old teddy bear, her favourite, and had returned empty-mouthed. Now he ran around Sandra, bouncing up at her; he ran towards the cutting and back again, barking.

The witch didn't like him, nor did he care for her. Once he had run into her grass only to emerge with his tail between his legs, while she watched through the grime, smiling like a skull. 'Keep that insect away from here, as well,' she shouted.

She shook her umbrella at him; it fluttered dangling like a sad broomstick. At once Mop pounced at it, barking. The girls tried to gag themselves with their knuckles, but vainly. Their laughter boiled up; they stood snorting helplessly, weeping with mirth.

The woman drew herself up rigidly; bony hands crept from her sleeves. The wizened apple turned slowly to Sandra, then to Debbie. The mouth was a thin bloodless slit full of teeth; the eyes seemed to have congealed around hatred. 'Well, you shouldn't have called him an insect,' Debbie said defensively.

Cars rushed by, two abreast. Shoppers hurried past, glancing at the woman and the two girls. Debbie could seize none of these distractions; she could only see the face. It wasn't a fruit or a vegetable now, it was a mask that had once been a face, drained of humanity. Its hatred was cold as a shark's gaze. Even the smallness of the face wasn't reassuring; it concentrated its power.

Mop bounced up and poked at the girls. At last they could turn; they ran. Their prams yawed. At the supermarket they looked back. The witch hadn't moved; the wizened mask stared above the immobile black coat. They stuck out their tongues, then they stalked home, nudging each other into nonchalance. 'She's only an old fart,' Debbie dared to say. In the street they stood and made faces at her house for minutes.

It wasn't long before Sandra came to ask Debbie to play. She couldn't have vacuumed so quickly, but perhaps she felt uneasy alone in the house. They played rounders in the street, with Lucy and her younger brother. Passing cars took sides.

When Debbie saw the witch approaching, a seed of fear grew in her stomach. But she was almost outside her own house; she needn't be afraid, even if the witch made faces at her again. Sandra must have thought similarly, for she ran across the pavement almost in front of the witch.

The woman didn't react; she seemed hardly to move. Only the black coat stirred a little as she passed, carrying her mask of hatred as though bearing it carefully somewhere, for a purpose. Debbie shouted for the ball; her voice clattered back from the houses, sounding false as her bravado.

As the witch reached her gate Miss Bake from the flats hurried over, blue hair glinting, hands fluttering. 'Oh, have they put the fire out?'

The witch peered suspiciously at her. 'I really couldn't tell you.'

'Haven't you heard?' This indifference made her more nervous; her voice leapt and shook. 'Some boys got into the houses by the supermarket and started a fire. That's what they told me at the corner. They

must have put it out. Isn't it wicked, Miss Trodden.
They never used to do these things. You can't feel
safe these days, can you?'

'Oh yes, I think I can.'

'You can't mean that, Miss Trodden. Nobody's safe,
not with all these children. If they're bored, why
doesn't someone give them something to do? The
churches should. They could find them something
worth doing. Someone's got to make the country safe
for the old folk.'

'Which churches are those?' She was smirking
faintly.

Miss Blake drew back a little. 'All the churches,'
she said, trying to placate her. 'All the Christians.
They should work together, form a coalition.'

'Oh, them. They've had their chance.' She smirked
broadly. 'Don't you worry. Someone will take control.
I must be going.'

Miss Bake hurried away, frowning and tutting; her
door slammed. Shortly the witch's face appeared
behind the grimy panes, glimmering as though twilight came earlier to her house. Her expression
lurked in the dimness, unreadable.

When Debbie's father called her in, she could tell
that her parents had had an argument; the flat was
heavy with dissatisfaction. 'When are you going trick-
or-treating?' her mother demanded.

'Tonight. After tea.'

'Well, you're not. You've got to go before it's dark.'

The argument was poised to pounce on Debbie.
'Oh, all right,' she said grumpily.

After lunch she washed up. Her father dabbed at
the plates, then sat watching football. He fiddled

irritably with the controls, but the flesh of the players grew orange. Her mother kept swearing at food as she prepared it. Debbie read her love comics, and tried to make herself invisible with silence. Through the wall she could hear the song of the vacuum droning about the flat in the next house.

Eventually it faded, and Sandra came knocking. 'You'd better go now,' Debbie's mother said.

'We're not going until tonight.'

'I'm sorry, Sandra, Debbie has to go before it's dark. And you aren't to go to anyone we don't know.'

'Oh, why not?' Sandra protested. Challenging strangers was part of the excitement. 'We won't go in,' Debbie said.

'Because you're not to, that's why.'

'Because some people have been putting things in sweets,' Debbie's father said wearily, hunching forward towards the television. 'Drugs and things. It was on the News.'

'You go with them,' her mother told him, worried again. 'Make sure they're all right.'

'What's stopping you?'

'You'll cook the tea, will you?'

'My mother might go,' Sandra said. 'But I think she's too tired.'

'Oh God, all right, I'll go. When the match is finished.' He slumped back in his armchair; the mock leather sighed. 'Never any bloody rest,' he muttered.

By the time they began it was dark, after all. But the streets weren't deserted and dimly exciting; they were full of people hurrying home from the match, shouting to each other, singing. Her father's impatience tugged at Debbie like a leash.

Some of the people they visited were preparing meals, and barely tolerant. Too many seemed anxious to trick them; perhaps they couldn't afford treats. At a teacher's house they had to attempt impossible plastic mazes which even Debbie's father decided irritably that he couldn't solve—though the teacher's wife sneaked them an apple each anyway. Elsewhere, several boys with glowing skulls for faces flung open a front door then slammed it, laughing. Mop appeared from an alley and joined the girls, to bounce at anyone who opened a door. He cheered Debbie, and she had pocketfuls of fruit and sweets. But it was an unsatisfying Hallowe'en.

They were nearly home when Mop began to growl. He baulked as they came abreast of the witch's garden. Unwillingly Debbie stared towards the house. The white mercury-vapour glare sharpened the tangled grass; a ragged spiky frieze of shadow lay low on the walls. The house seemed smoky and dim, drained of colour. But she could see the gaping doorway, the coat like a tent of darker shadow, the dim perched face, a hand beckoning. 'Come here,' the voice said. 'I've got something for you.'

'Go on, be quick,' hissed Debbie's father.

The girls hesitated. 'Go on, she won't bite you,' he said, pushing Debbie. 'Take it while she's offering.'

He wanted peace, he wanted her to make friends with the old witch. If she said she was frightened he would only tell her not to be stupid. Now he had made her more frightened to refuse. She dragged her feet up the cracked path, towards the door to shadow. Dangling grasses plucked at her socks, scraping dryly. The house stretched her shadow into its mouth.

Fists like knotted clubs crept from sleeves and deposited something in Debbie's palm, then in Sandra's: wrapped boiled sweets. 'There you are,' said the shrunken mouth, smiling dimly.

'Thank you very much.' Debbie almost screamed: she hadn't heard her father follow her, to thank the woman. His finger was trying to prod her to gratitude.

'Let's see if you like them,' the witch said.

Debbie's fingers picked stiffly at the wrapping. The paper rustled like the dead grass, loud and somehow vicious. She raised the bared sweet towards her mouth, wondering whether she could drop it. She held her mouth still around the sweet. But when she could no longer fend off the taste, it was pleasant: raspberry, clear and sharp. 'It's nice,' she said. 'Thank you.'

'Yes, it is,' Sandra said.

Hearing her voice Mop, who had halted snarling at the far end of the path, came racing between the clattering grasses. 'We mustn't forget the dog, must we,' the voice said. Mop overshot his sweet and bounced back to catch it. Sandra made to run to him, but he'd crunched and swallowed the sweet. They turned back to the house. The closed front door faced them in the dimness.

'I'm going home now,' Sandra said and ran into her house, followed by Mop. Debbie found an odd taste in her mouth: a thick bitter trail, as if something had crawled down her throat. Just the liquid centre of the sweet: it wasn't worth telling her father, he would only be impatient. 'Did you enjoy yourself?' he said, tousling her hair, and she nodded.

During the meal her tongue searched for the taste.

It was never there, nor could she find it in her memory; perhaps it hadn't been there at all. She watched comedies on television; she was understanding more of the jokes that made her parents laugh. She tricked some little girls who came to the door, but they looked so forlorn that she gave them sweets. The street was bare, deserted, frosted by the light: the ghost of its daytime self. She was glad to close it out. She watched the screen. Colours bobbed up, laughter exploded; gaps interrupted, for she was falling asleep. 'Do you want to go to bed? She strained to prove she didn't but at last admitted to herself that she did. In bed she fell asleep at once.

She slept uneasily. Something kept waking her: a sound, a taste? Straining drowsily to remember, she drifted into sleep. Once she glimpsed a figure staring at her from the doorway—her father. Only seconds later—or so it seemed at first—she woke again. A face had peered in the window. She turned violently, tethered by the blankets. There was nothing but the lighted gap which she always left between the curtains, to keep her company in the dark. The house was silent, asleep.

Her mind streamed with thoughts. The mask on the wizened apple, the skull-faced boys, the street flattened by the glare, her father's finger prodding her ribs. The face that had peered in her window had been hanging wide, too wide. It was the melting monkey from when she was little. Placing it didn't reassure her. The house surrounded her, huge and unfamiliar, darkly threatening.

She tried to think of Mop. He ran barking into the tunnel—no, he chased cheekily around the witch.

Debbie remembered the day he had run into the witch's garden. Scared to pursue him, they had watched him vanish amid the grass. They'd heard digging, then a silence: what sounded like a pattering explosion of earth, a threshing of grass, and Mop had run out with his tail between his legs. The dim face had watched, grinning.

That wasn't reassuring either. She tried to think of something she loved, but could think of nothing but her old bear that Mop had stolen. Her mind became a maze, leading always back to the face at her window. She'd seen it only once, but she had often felt it peering in. Its jaw had sagged like wax, pulling open a yawning pink throat. She had been ill, she must have been frightened by a monkey making a face on television. But as the mouth had drooped and then drawn up again, she'd heard a voice speaking to her through the glass: a slow deep dragging voice that sagged like the face, stretching out each separate word. She'd lain paralysed as the voice blurred in the glass, but hadn't been able to make out a word. She opened her eyes to dislodge the memory. A shadow sprang away from the window.

Only a car's light, plucking at the curtains. She lay, trying to be calm around her heart. But she felt uneasy, and kept almost tasting the centre of the burst sweet. The room seemed oppressive; she felt imprisoned. The window imprisoned her, for something could peer in.

She crawled out of bed. The floor felt unpleasantly soft underfoot, as if mouldering in the dark. The street stretched below, deserted and glittering; the witch's windows were black, as though the grime had filled the house. The taste was almost in Debbie's mouth.

Had the witch put something in the sweets? Suddenly Debbie had to know whether Sandra had tasted it too. She had to shake off the oppressively padded darkness. She dressed, fumbling quietly in the dark. Squirming into her anorak, she crept into the hall. She couldn't leave the front door open, the wind would slam it. She tiptoed into the living-room and groped in her mother's handbag. Her face burned; it skulked dimly in the mirror. She clutched the key in her fist and inched open the door to the stairs.

On the stairs she realised she was behaving stupidly. How could she waken Sandra without disturbing her mother? Sandra's bedroom window faced the back yard, too far from the alley to pelt. Yet her thoughts seemed only a commentary, for she was still descending. She opened the front door, and started. Sandra was waiting beneath the streetlamp.

She was wearing her anorak too. She looked anxious. 'Mop's run off,' she said.

'Oh no . . . Shall we look for him?'

'Come on, I know where he is.' They muffled their footsteps, which sounded like a dream. The bleached street stood frozen around them, fossilised by the glare; trees cast nets over the houses, cars squatted, closed and dim. The ghost of the street made Debbie dislike to ask, but she had to know. 'Do you think she put something funny in those sweets? Did you taste something?'

'Yes, I can now.' At once Debbie could too: a brief hint of the indefinable taste. She hadn't wanted so definite an answer: she bit her lip.

At the main road Sandra turned towards the super-market. Shops displayed bare slabs of glazed light, plastic cups scuttled in the underpass. How could Sandra be so sure where Mop had gone? Why did Debbie feel she knew as well? Sandra ran past the supermarket. Surely they weren't going to—But Sandra was already running into an alley, towards the cutting.

She gazed down, waiting for Debbie. White lamps glared into the artificial valley; shadows of the broken walls crumbled over scattered bricks. 'He won't have gone down there,' Debbie said, wanting to believe it. 'He has,' Sandra cried. 'Listen.'

The wind wandered groping among the clutter on the tracks, it hooted feebly in the stone throat. Another sound was floated up to Debbie by the wind, then snatched away: a whining?

'He's in the tunnel,' Sandra said. 'Come on.'

She slipped down a few feet; her face stared over the edge at Debbie. 'If you don't come you aren't my friend,' she said.

Debbie watched her reach the floor of the cutting and stare up challengingly; then reluctantly she followed. A bitter taste rose momentarily in her throat. She slithered down all too swiftly. The dark deep tunnel grew tall.

Why didn't Sandra call? 'Mop! Mop!' Debbie shouted. But her shouted dropped into the cutting like pats of mud. There might have been an answering whine; the wind threw the sound away. 'Come on,' Sandra said impatiently.

She strode into the tunnel. The shadow hanging from the arch chopped her in half, then wiped her out entirely. Debbie remembered the little boy who had vanished. Suppose he were in there now—what would he be like? Around her the glistening cartons shifted restlessly; their gaping tops nodded. Twisted skeletons rattled, jangling.

Some of the squealing of metal might be an animal's faint cry; perhaps the metal was what they'd heard. 'All right,' Sandra said from the dark, 'you're not my friend.'

Debbie glanced about hopelessly. A taste touched her mouth. Above her, ruins gleamed jaggedly against the sky; cartons dipped their mouths towards her, torn lips working. Among piled bricks at the edge of the cutting, a punctured football or a crumpled rag peered down at her. Unwillingly she walked forward.

Darkness fell on her, filling her eyes. 'Wait until your eyes get used to it,' Sandra said, but Debbie disliked to keep them closed for long. At last bricks began to solidify from the dark. Darkness arched over her, outlines of bricks glinted faintly. The rails were thin dull lines, shortly erased by the dark.

Sandra groped forward. 'Go slowly, then we won't fall over anything,' she said.

They walked slowly as a dream, halting every few feet to wait for the light to catch up. Debbie's eyes were full of shifting fog which fastened very gradually on her surroundings, sketching them: the dwindling arch of the tunnel, the fading rails. Her progress was like a ritual in a nightmare.

The first stretch of the tunnel was cluttered with missiles: broken bottles crunched underfoot, tin cans toppled loudly. After that the way was clear, except for odd lurking bricks. But the dark was oppressively full of the sounds the girls made—hasty breathing, shuffling, the chafing of rust against their feet—and Debbie could never be sure whether, amid the close sounds and the invisibility, there was a whining.

They shuffled onward. Cold encircled them, dripping. The tunnel smelled dank and dusty; it seemed to insinuate a bitter taste into Debbie's mouth. She felt the weight of earth huge around the stone tube. The dimness flickered forward again, beckoning them on. It was almost as though someone were coaxing them into the tunnel with a feeble lamp. Beneath her feet bricks scraped and clattered.

The twilight flickered, then leapt ahead. The roundness of the tunnel glistened faintly; Debbie could make out random edges of brick, a dull hint of rails. The taste grew in her mouth. Again she felt that they were being led. She didn't dare ask Sandra whether the light was really moving. It must be her eyes. A shadow loomed on the arch overhead: the bearer of the light—behind her. She turned gasping. At once the dimness went out. The distant mouth of the tunnel was small as a fingernail.

Its light couldn't have reached so far. Something else had illuminated their way. The taste filled her mouth, like suffocation; dark dripped all around her; the distant entrance flickered, dancing. If she made for the entrance Sandra would have to follow. She could move now, she'd only to move one foot, just one, just a little. Sandra screamed.

When Debbie turned—furious with Sandra: there was nothing to be scared of, they could go now, escape—shadows reached for her. The light had leapt ahead again, still dim but brighter. The shadows were attached to vague objects, of which the nearest seemed familiar. Light gathered on it, crawling, glimmering. It had large ragged ears. It was her old lost teddy bear.

It was moving. In the subterranean twilight its fur stirred as it drowned. No, it wasn't the fur. Debbie's bear was covered with a swarm that crawled. The swarm was emerging sluggishly from within the bear, piling more thickly on its body, crawling.

It was a lost toy, not hers at all. Nothing covered it but moisture and unstable light. 'It's all right,' she muttered weakly. 'It's only someone's old bear.' But Sandra was staring beyond it, sobbing with horror.

Farther in, where dimness and dark flickered together, there was a hole in the floor of the tunnel, surrounded by bricks and earth and something that squatted. It squatted at the edge; its hands dangled into the hole, its dim face gaped pinkly. Its eyes gleamed like bubbles of mud.

'Oh, oh,' Sandra sobbed. 'It's the monkey.'

Perhaps that was the worst—that Sandra knew the gaping face too. But Debbie's horror was blurred and numbing, because she could see so much. She could see what lay beside the hole, struggling feebly as if drugged, and whining: Mop.

Sandra staggered towards him as if she had lost her balance. Debbie stumbled after her, unable to think, feeling only her feet dragging her over the jagged floor. Then part of the darkness shifted and advanced on them, growing paler. A toy—a large clockwork toy, jerking rustily: the figure of a little boy, its body and ragged sodden clothes covered with dust and cobwebs. It plodded jerkily between them and the hole, and halted. Parts of it shone white, as if patched with flaking paint: particularly the face.

Debbie tried to look away, to turn, to run. But the taste burned in her mouth; it seemed to thread her with a rigid frame, holding her helpless. The dim stone tube was hemmed in by darkness; the twilight fluttered. Dust crawled in her throat. The toy bear glistened restlessly. The figure of the little boy swayed; its face glimmered, pale, featureless, blotchy. The monkey moved.

Its long hands closed around Mop and pulled him into the hole, then they scooped bricks and earth on top of him. The earth struggled in the hole, the whining became a muffled coughing and choking. Eventually the earth was still. The squat floppy body capered on the grave. Thick deep laughter, very slow, dropped from the gaping face. Each time the jaw drooped lower, almost touching the floor.

Another part of the dark moved. 'That'll teach you. You won't forget that,' a voice said.

It was the witch. She was lurking in the darkness, out of sight. Her voice was as lifeless now as her face had been. Debbie was able to see that the woman needed to hide in the dark to be herself. But she was trapped too efficiently for the thought to be at all reassuring.

'You'd better behave yourselves in future. I'll be watching,' the voice said. 'Go on now. Go away.'

As Debbie found she was able to turn, though very lethargically, the little boy moved. She heard a crack; then he seemed to shrink jerkily, and topple towards her. But she was turning, and saw no more. The taste was heavy in her. She couldn't run; she could only plod through the close treacherous darkness towards the tiny light.

The light refused to grow. She plodded, she plodded, but the light held itself back. Then at last it seemed nearer, and much later it reached into the dark. She plodded out, exhausted and hollow. She clambered numbly up the bank, dragged her feet through the deserted streets; she was just aware of Sandra near her. She climbed the stairs, slipped the key into the handbag, went into her room, still trudging. Her numb trudge became the plodding of her heart, her slow suffocated gasps. She woke.

So it had been a dream, after all. Her mouth tasted bitter. What had awakened her? She lay uneasily, eyelids tight, trying to retreat into sleep; if she awoke completely she'd be alone with the dark. But light flapped on her eyelids. Something was wrong. The room was too bright, and flickering. Things cracked loudly, popping; a voice cried her name. Reluctantly she groped to the window, towards the blazing light.

The witch's house was on fire. Flames gushed from the windows, painting smoke red. Sandra stood outside, crying 'Debbie!' As Debbie watched, bewildered, a screaming blaze appeared at an upstairs window, jerking like a puppet; then it writhed and fell back into the flames. Sandra seemed to be dancing, outlined by reflected fire, and weeping.

People were unlocking doors. Sandra's mother hurried out, and Debbie's father. Sandra's mother fluttered about, trying to drag the girl home, but Sandra was crying 'Debbie!' Debbie gripped the sill, afraid to let go.

More houses were switched on. Debbie's mother ran out. There was a hasty discussion among the parents, then Debbie's father came hurrying back with Sandra. Debbie dodged into bed as they came upstairs; the witch's house roared, splintering.

'Here's Sandra, Debbie. She's frightened. She's going to sleep with you tonight.' Shadows rushed into the room with him. When Sandra took off her dressing-gown and stood holding it, confused, he threw it impatiently on the chair. 'Into bed now, quickly. And just you stay there.'

They heard him hurrying downstairs, Sandra's mother saying, 'Oh God, oh my God,' Debbie's mother trying to calm her down. The girls lay silent in the shaking twilit room. Sandra was trembling.

'What happened?' Debbie whispered. 'Did you see?'

After a while Sandra sobbed. 'My little dog,' she said indistinctly.

Was that an answer? Debbie's thoughts were blurred; the room quaked, Sandra's dressing-gown was slipping off the chair, distracting her. 'What about Mop?' she whispered. 'Where is he?'

Sandra seemed to be choking. The dressing-gown fell in a heap on the floor. Debbie felt nervous. What had happened to Mop? She'd dreamed—Surely Sandra couldn't have dreamed that too. The rest of the contents of the chair were following the dressing-gown.

'I dreamed,' Debbie began uneasily, and bitterness filled her mouth like a gag. When she'd finished choking, she had forgotten what she'd meant to say. The room and furniture were unsteady with dimming light. Far away and fading, she heard her parents' voices.

Sandra was trying to speak. 'Debbie,' she said, 'Debbie.' Her body shook violently, with effort or with fear. 'I burned the witch,' she said. 'Because of what she did.'

Debbie stared in front of her, aghast. She couldn't take in Sandra's words. Too much had happened too quickly: the dream, the fire, her own bitter-tasting dumbness. Sandra's revelation, the distracting object that drooped from the chair— But until Sandra's dressing-gown was thrown there, that chair had been empty.

She heard Sandra's almost breathless cry. Something dim squatted forward on the chair. Its pink yawning drooped towards the floor. Very slowly, relishing each separate word, it began to speak.

*   *   *

RAMSEY CAMPBELL, Britain's leading writer of weird stories, wrote his first tale, 'Black Fingers from Space', in a red school exercise book when he was not quite eight years old. Long before that he had learnt all about being frightened, when he read the story by Hans Christian Andersen about the little girl who cuts off her feet to rid herself of her red dancing shoes. By the time he was eleven he had finished a short book of ghost and horror stories which, he says, 'was patched together like Frankenstein's monster from fragments of tales I had read.' By 1964 *The Inhabitant of the Lake*, his book of stories imitating the work of the important and influential writer H.P.

Lovecraft, had been published in America, and soon afterwards his short stories on various ghoulish themes were winning him admirers in Britain. His fascination with childhood is clear in novels like *The Doll Who Ate his Mother* and *The Nameless*, and many of his later short stories have featured young, alienated and often selfish youngsters who are neither evil nor innocent, merely victims. Several of these have been highly praised, including 'Eyes of Childhood', 'Bedtime Story' and the prizewinning 'In the Bag'. Ramsey Campbell said recently, 'Perhaps the reason I often return to the theme is that deep down we are all still as vulnerable as we were in childhood.'

A TOY FOR JULIETTE

Robert Bloch

Juliette lives in the future, but in some respects she's not so different from girls today. She is pretty, on the verge of womanhood, and still excited by the presents her grandfather brings her whenever he goes on a trip. The old man's journeys are of the kind we can only dream about today—travels in time—and the toys that he brings back for Juliette are often very out of the ordinary . . . like a torture rack, a pair of stocks, and a grotesque Iron Maiden of Nuremberg in which sharp spikes crush anyone inside to death. But this time, Grandfather has brought something even more scary— a real live toy . . .

*　　*　　*

Juliette entered her bedroom, smiling, and a thousand Juliettes smiled back at her. For all the walls were panelled with mirrors, and the ceiling was set with inlaid panes that reflected her image.

Wherever she glanced she could see the blonde curls framing the sensitive features of a face that was a radiant amalgam of both child and angel; a striking contrast to the rich, ripe revelation of her body in the filmy robe.

But Juliette wasn't smiling at herself. She smiled because she knew that Grandfather was back, and he'd brought her another toy. In just a few moments it would be decontaminated and delivered, and she wanted to be ready.

Juliette turned the ring on her finger and the mirrors dimmed. Another turn would darken the room entirely; a twist in the opposite direction would bring them blazing into brilliance. It was all a matter of choice—but then, that was the secret of life. To choose, for pleasure.

And what was her pleasure tonight?

Juliette advanced to one of the mirror panels and passed her hand before it. The glass slid to one side, revealing the niche behind it; the coffin-shaped opening in the solid rock, with the boot and thumbscrews set at the proper heights.

For a moment she hesitated; she hadn't played *that* game in years. Another time, perhaps. Juliette waved her hand and the mirror moved to cover the opening again.

She wandered along the row of panels, gesturing as she walked, pausing to inspect what was behind each mirror in turn. Here was the rack, there the stocks with the barbed whips resting against the dark-stained wood. And here was the dissecting table, hundreds of years old, with its quaint instruments; behind the next panel, the electrical prods and wires that produced such weird grimaces and contortions of agony, to say nothing of screams. Of course the screams didn't matter in a soundproofed room.

Juliette moved to the side wall and waved her hand again; the obedient glass slid away and she stared at a plaything she'd almost forgotten. It was one of the first things Grandfather had ever given her, and it was very old, almost like a mummy case. What had he called it? The Iron Maiden of Nuremberg, that was it—with the sharpened steel spikes set inside the lid. You chained a man inside, and you turned the little crank that closed the lid, ever so slowly, and the spikes pierced the wrists and the elbows, the ankles and the knees, the groin and the eyes. You had to be careful not to get excited and turn too quickly, or you'd spoil the fun.

Grandfather had shown her how it worked, the first time he brought her a real *live* toy. But then, Grandfather had shown her everything. He'd taught her all she knew, for he was very wise. He'd even given her her name—Juliette—from one of the old-fashioned printed books he'd discovered by the philosopher De Sade.

Grandfather had brought the books from the Past, just as he'd brought the playthings for her. He was the only one who had access to the Past, because he owned the Traveller.

The Traveller was a very ingenious mechanism, capable of attaining vibrational frequencies which freed it from the time-bind. At rest, it was just a big square boxlike shape, the size of a small room. But when Grandfather took over the controls and the oscillation started, the box would blur and disappear. It was still there, Grandfather said—at least, the *matrix* remained as a fixed point in space and time— but anything or anyone within the square could move freely into the Past to wherever the controls were programmed. Of course they would be invisible when they arrived, but that was actually an advantage, par- ticularly when it came to finding things and bringing them back. Grandfather had brought back some very interesting objects from almost mythical places—the great library of Alexandria, the Pyramid of Cheops, the Kremlin, the Vatican, Fort Knox—all the storehouses of treasure and knowledge which existed thousands of years ago. He liked to go to *that* part of the Past, the period before the thermonuclear wars and the robotic ages, and collect things. Of course, books and jewels and metals were useless, except to an antiquarian, but Grandfather was a romanticist and loved the olden times.

It was strange to think of him owning the Traveller, but of course he hadn't actually created it. Juliette's father was really the one who built it, and Grandfather took possession of it after her father died. Juliette suspected Grandfather had killed her father and mother when she was just a baby, but she could never be sure. Not that it mattered; Grandfather was always very good to her, and besides, soon he would die and she'd own the Traveller herself.

They used to joke about it frequently. 'I've made you into a monster,' he'd say. 'And someday you'll end up by destroying me. After which, of course, you'll go on to destroy the entire world—or what little remains of it.'

'Aren't you afraid?' she'd tease.

'Certainly not. That's my dream—the destruction of everything. An end to all this sterile decadence. Do you realise that at one time there were more than three billion inhabitants on this planet? And now, less than three thousand! Less than three thousand, shut up inside these Domes; prisoners of themselves and sealed away forever, thanks to the sins of the father who poisoned not only the outside world but outer space by meddling with the atomic order of the universe. Humanity is virtually extinct already; you will merely hasten the finale.'

'But couldn't we all go back to another time, in the Traveller?' she asked.

'Back to *what* time? The continuum is changeless; one event leads inexorably to another, all links in a chain which binds us to the present and its inevitable end in destruction. We'd have temporary individual survival, yes, but to no purpose. And none of us are fitted to survive in a more primitive environment. So let us stay here and take what pleasure we can from the moment. *My* pleasure is to be the sole user and possessor of the Traveller. And yours, Juliette—'

Grandfather laughed then. They both laughed, because they knew what *her* pleasure was.

Juliette killed her first toy when she was eleven— a little boy. It had been brought to her as a special gift from Grandfather, from somewhere in the Past, for elementary sex play. But it wouldn't cooperate, and she lost her temper and beat it to death with a steel rod. So Grandfather brought her an older toy, with brown skin, and it cooperated very well, but in the end she tired of it and one day when it was sleeping in her bed she tied it down and found a knife.

Experimenting a little before it died, Juliette discovered new sources of pleasure, and of course Grandfather found out. That's when he'd christened her 'Juliette'; he seemed to approve most highly, and from then on he brought her the playthings she kept behind the mirrors in her bedroom. And on his restless rovings into the Past he brought her new toys.

Being invisible, he could find them for her almost anywhere on his travels—all he did was to use a stunner and transport them when he returned. Of course each toy had to be very carefully decontaminated; the Past was teeming with strange microorganisms. But once the toys were properly antiseptic they were turned over to Juliette for her pleasure, and during the past seven years she had enjoyed herself.

It was always delicious, this moment of anticipation before a new toy arrived. What would it be like? Grandfather was most considerate; mainly, he made sure that the toys he brought her could speak and understand Anglish—or 'English', as they used to call it in the Past. Verbal communication was often important, particularly if Juliette wanted to follow the precepts of the philosopher De Sade and enjoy some form of sex relation before going on to keener pleasures.

But there was still the guessing beforehand. Would this toy be young or old, wild or tame, male or female? She'd had all kinds, and every possible combination. Sometimes she kept them alive for days before tiring of them—or before the subtleties of which she was capable caused them to expire. At other times she wanted it to happen quickly; tonight, for example, she knew she could be soothed only by the most primitive and direct action.

Once Juliette realised this, she stopped playing with her mirror panels and went directly to the big bed. She pulled back the coverlet, groped under the pillow until she felt it. Yes, it was still there—the big knife with the long, cruel blade. She knew what she would do now: take the toy to bed with her and then,

at precisely the proper moment, combine her pleasures. If she could time her knife thrust—

She shivered with anticipation, then with impatience.

What kind of toy would it be? She remembered the
suave, cool one—Benjamin Bathurst was his name, an
English diplomat from the time of what Grandfather
called the Napoleonic Wars. Oh, he'd been suave and
cool enough, until she beguiled him with her body,
into the bed. And there'd been that American aviatrix
from slightly later on in the Past, and once, as a very
special treat, the entire crew of a sailing vessel called
the *Marie Celeste*. They had lasted for *weeks!*

Strangely enough, she'd even read about some of
her toys afterwards. Because when Grandfather
approached them with his stunner and brought them
here, they disappeared forever from the Past, and if
they were in any way known or important in their
time, such disappearances were noted. And some of
Grandfather's books had accounts of the 'mysterious
vanishing' which took place and was, of course, never
explained. How delicious it all was!

Juliette patted the pillow back into place and slid
the knife under it. She couldn't wait, now; what was
delaying things?

She forced herself to move to a vent and depress
the sprayer, shedding her robe as the perfumed mist
bathed her body. It was the final allurement—but
why didn't her toy arrive?

Suddenly Grandfather's voice came over the
auditor.

'I'm sending you a little surprise, dearest.'

That's what he always said: it was part of the game.

Juliette depressed the communicator-taggle. 'Don't tease,' she begged. 'Tell me what it's like.'

'An Englishman. Late Victorian Era. Very prim and proper, by the looks of him.'

'Young? Handsome?'

'Passsable.' Grandfather chuckled. 'Your appetites betray you, dearest.'

'Who is it—someone from the books?'

'I wouldn't know the name. We found no identification during the decontamination. But from his dress and manner, and the little black bag he carried when I discovered him so early in the morning, I'd judge him to be a physician returning from an emergency call.'

Juliette knew about 'physicians' from her reading of course; just as she knew what 'Victorian' meant. Somehow the combination seemed exactly right.

'Prim and proper?' She giggled. 'Then I'm afraid it's due for a shock.'

Grandfather laughed. 'You have something in mind, I take it?'

'Yes.'

'Can I watch?'

'Please—not this time.'

'Very well.'

'Don't be mad, darling. I love you.'

Juliette switched off. Just in time, too, because the door was opening and the toy came in.

She stared at it, realising that Grandfather had told the truth. The toy was a male of thirty-odd years, attractive but by no means handsome. It couldn't be, in that dark garb and those ridiculous side whiskers. There was something almost depressingly refined and mannered about it, an air of embarrassed repression.

And of course, when it caught sight of Juliette in her revealing robe, and the bed surrounded by mirrors, it actually began to *blush*.

That reaction won Juliette completely. A blushing Victorian, with the build of a bull—and unaware that this was the slaughterhouse!

It was so amusing she couldn't restrain herself; she moved forward at once and put her arms around it.

'Who—who are you? Where am I?'

The usual questions, voiced in the usual way. Ordinarily, Juliette would have amused herself by parrying with answers designed to tantalise and titillate her victim. But tonight she felt an urgency which only increased as she embraced the toy and pressed it back towards the waiting bed.

The toy began to breathe heavily, responding. But it was still bewildered. 'Tell me—I don't understand. Am I alive? Or is this heaven?'

Juliette's robe fell open as she lay back. 'You're alive, darling,' she murmured. 'Wonderfully alive.' She laughed as she began to prove the statement. 'But closer to heaven than you think.'

And to prove *that* statement, her free hand slid under the pillow and groped for the waiting knife.

But the knife wasn't there any more. Somehow it had already found its way into the toy's hand. And the toy wasn't prim and proper any longer, its face was something glimpsed in nightmare. Just a glimpse, before the blinding blur of the knife blade, as it came down, again and again and again—

The room, of course, was soundproof, and there was plenty of time. They didn't discover what was left of Juliette's body for several days.

Back in London, after the final mysterious murder in the early morning hours, they never did find Jack the Ripper . . .

*   *   *

ROBERT BLOCH is the author of two of the most famous tales about Jack the Ripper: a short story, 'Yours Truly, Jack the Ripper', in which the notorious killer has become immortal as a result of his evil deeds, and a novel, *The Night of the Ripper*, in which the mysterious figure is finally revealed to have been a *woman*!

As a child in Maywood, Illinois, Bloch was a great reader, the leader of the neighbourhood gang, and 'cowardly, treacherous, cruel, stubborn, unreasonable, vain, selfish and hysterical—in short, just like any other kid.' Like Ramsey Campbell, he began his writing career imitating the stories of H.P. Lovecraft, but he first startled readers when he was just 17 by contributing a really gruesome story about cannibalism, 'The Feast in the Abbey', to the magazine *Weird Tales*. In 1959 he became known all over the world for his novel *Psycho*, which was made into a famous film by Alfred Hitchcock.

Although Robert Bloch wrote a lot of really scary tales about children, including 'A Lesson for the Teacher', 'The Bat is my Brother' and 'Groovyland', he was one of the nicest and gentlest people you could wish to meet—although he did like joking that he had 'the brain of a small boy . . . which I keep in a jar!'

ACKNOWLEDGEMENTS

The editor is grateful to the following authors, publishers and agents for permission to include copyright stories in this collection: Scholastic Inc. for 'The Spell' by R.L.Stine; the author for 'It's a Good Life' by Jerome Bixby; Abner Stein Ltd for 'Drink My Red Blood' by Richard Matheson and 'The Man Upstairs' by Ray Bradbury; the author for 'Something Nasty' by William F. Nolan; Winant Towers Ltd for 'The Restless Ghost' by Leon Garfield; Davis Publications Inc. for 'The Thirteenth Day of Christmas' by Isaac Asimov; Avon Books for 'Hush!' by Zenna Henderson; David Higham Associates for 'Spotty Powder' by Roald Dahl; Victor Gollancz Ltd for 'Dead Language Master' by Joan Aiken; Little Brown for 'Here There Be Tygers' by Stephen King; the author for 'The Trick' by Ramsey Campbell; and Mrs Ellie Bloch for 'A Toy for Juliette' by Robert Bloch. While every care has been taken to clear permission for the use of the stories in this collection, in the case of any accidental infringement, copyright holders are asked to write to the editor care of the publishers.